"It's missing! My masterpiece is missing!" Poppa cried.

"There's only one explanation," said Bertram, feeling suddenly bold. "The X-13 must have worked."

"What?" asked Poppa.

"The X-13," Bertram repeated. "You must have gotten the formula right after all."

"What are you talking about?" Poppa asked. "I didn't use any X-13 in the statue of The Man Being Boiled Alive."

"No, but *I* did," said Bertram with a sense of triumph. "I slipped some into the mixture. I had faith in you, and I knew if we just gave the formula another chance, it would work."

"This is awful!" Poppa exclaimed.

"I know," Bertram agreed. "Especially since the town meeting is tonight. If the statue escapes from this museum, who knows what it'll do?"

FEAR FACTORY

#1

The Trouble
With Formula X-13

Marc Gave

PRICE STERN SLOAN
Los Angeles

ISBN: 0-8431-2709-0

10   9   8   7   6   5   4   3   2   1

— One —

"Shhh!" Bertram Potter put his finger to his lips and nodded toward the heavy oak door that separated the laboratory where he and his grandfather were sitting, from his living room.

At once, Poppa stopped reading his book of magic aloud and raised his head. He frowned, as if he doubted his eleven-year-old grandson.

"I'm serious. My parents are coming," Bertram whispered, annoyed. "I have the hearing of a bat, remember?"

"You told me we'd be safe for three hours," Poppa whispered back.

"So I was wrong," Bertram said. "Let's get out of here."

"This is *my* lab," Poppa argued. "It's okay for me to be here. You're the one who has to leave."

But Bertram knew perfectly well that his grandfather was only joking.

"All right. Let's put away this stuff and get out of here," Poppa said with a wink. He nimbly made his way over to the far wall and put some jars full of colored liquids back on the

1

shelf. "We can finish our experiment later. Maybe tonight."

Betram nodded. "I'll try to come down sometime after ten o'clock. It's just that Mom and Dad would kill me if they knew I came down here without finishing my social studies homework first," Bertram said. "I'm supposed to be at Wesley's doing a flour and water map of the United States."

"Okay," Poppa agreed as they left the lab and locked the door behind them. "But you know your parents wouldn't want you down here with me even if you had finished your social studies for the entire year. They think I'm a bad influence or something." He chuckled. "Sooner or later, though, they'll have to admit that magic is in your blood. For now, we'll just have to be patient. Their minds are so busy with profit-and-loss statements, they forget that if I don't train you properly, there will be no one to take over when I'm gone."

"Don't talk like that, Poppa," Bertram said, turning around to face his grandfather. "You still look young. You're going to live to be a hundred and twenty years old, at least."

Bertram and Poppa walked out of Poppa's apartment and casually strolled through the halls of the huge brick building that was their home as well as the family business — a wax museum known as the Fear Factory. Bertram hoped they looked like they were taking an innocent little walk.

"Uh-oh," Poppa muttered as they started up the stairs from the ground floor. "Looks like we have a welcoming committee."

Bertram's parents, Clark and Marie Potter, were standing at the top of the stairs, waiting for them. Bertram's father, wearing a striped tie and a white shirt with the collar button open and the sleeves rolled up, folded his arms across his chest. Behind his horned-rimmed glasses, his eyes had that "I-can't-believe-you've-done-it-again" look. Bertram's mother was tapping one foot impatiently.

"Hi, guys," Bertram said coolly. He knew they knew he hadn't been at his best friend Wesley's house slaving over a flour and water map.

"Poppa," Bertram's dad said, "we're on to you. I know you two were just in the lab. It's hard enough to raise a kid without my own father teaching him to be a sneak. You ought to know better."

"I can learn more in Poppa's lab than from making an old map," Bertram said. "Besides, Wesley said I'd only spoil it."

"We figured something was up," Bertram's mother said. "Mrs. Fairchild called and asked if she could send Wesley over because his sisters have to rehearse for their ballet recital."

"Yuck," Wesley complained, coming up behind Mrs. Potter. "They'll have to practice their whole lives to be half as good as those dancing chimps who came to our school last year. But my mom says I have to go see Creep One and Creep Two at their stupid recital. She thinks it'll expose me to the finer things in life. If those sisters of mine are two of the finer things, then count me out!" Wesley exclaimed. "Hey, what's for dessert, Mrs. Potter? Mom said I could have it here."

"Come along, Wesley. Dora made chocolate mud pie."

"What a waste of flour," Bertram said as he and Wesley mixed up the white pasty mess for their map that night after dinner. "I'd rather make a cake. Maybe Dora will show us how after we finish this."

"*If* we finish. What's taking you so long to stir that glop?"

"It's sticking to the spoon," Bertram said.

At that moment the cook stuck her head into the dining room, where the boys were working. "Did I hear my name bein' taken in vain?" she asked with a throaty laugh.

"I said that maybe when we were finished, you'd show us something better to do with flour than making this stupid map," Bertram replied.

"By the time you're finished with that, all you'll be fit for is a good hosing down," Dora said. "You're starting to look like one of your grandfather's waxworks."

Bertram caught a glimpse of himself in the dining room mirror. Flour had settled in his dark brown hair and there was a white smudge across his freckled nose. His clothes were also covered with a fine dusting of flour. Wesley, on the other hand, was perfectly clean, because he hadn't helped with the project at all.

"Let's call it done, huh?" Wesley suggested.

"One final stir," Bertram said. "I'll make it a big one."

Bertram had been stirring the mixture for a long time. He dug the long-handled wooden spoon in so deeply that it stuck fast. Just as he began to pull it out of the bowl his cat, Fishbreath, decided to chase a moth that was flitting by. The huge orange tomcat took a leap right into Bertram, knocking him off balance. His hand slipped from the rim of the bowl. Instead of the spoon coming out of the bowl, the bowl stuck to it, and landed, along with Bertram, on the dining room floor.

"Uh, I think it's time for me to go home now," Wesley said, peering at Bertram from under the table. Thick flour and water paste was running down the sides of Bertram's face.

"You might ask a guy if he's hurt," Bertram said angrily.

"Gleep," said Wesley.

"That alien stuff isn't funny any more," Bertram said. "If you're not going to help me, why *don't* you go home?"

"'Bye, Dora," Wesley called into the kitchen. Then he left the room and thudded down the steps, leaving Bertram to clean up the mess and do the explaining.

While he was scraping flour paste off the rug, Bertram wondered why he put up with Wesley.

The next evening, Bertram made a big show of going to his room and closing the door loudly.

Then he noiselessly reopened it and tiptoed past the living room. His parents were watching the first of six old television shows from the 1950s that they had discovered they couldn't live without since they got cable. Bertram thought it was pretty sad that after having actually spent their childhood watching the same shows, they would want to watch them again. But it did give him nearly three hours to spend in Poppa's lab!

He couldn't understand why his parents didn't want their only son to follow in his grandfather's footsteps. If it weren't for Poppa and his way with wax figures, they wouldn't have a business to manage. What would happen to the Fear Factory if Bertram took piano lessons and went to business school the way they wanted? Who would take over from Poppa when he got too old?

He couldn't imagine they'd want Sigmund von Breymer, Poppa's assistant, for a partner. Although he had known Siggy all his life, and Siggy was terrific at making the statues, Bertram couldn't help admitting to himself that there was something creepy about the guy, too creepy even for him. Bertram stepped off the bottom step onto the first floor — the museum floor. Using a flashlight, he made his way along the familiar corridors of the Hall of Monsters, through the Rooms of Blood, and on into the Chambers of Doom. Behind that goriest of gory sections of the wax museum, he came to the storage area that served as the reception room for his grandfather's apartment.

He knocked four times — one long and three short — at the heavy oak door that led into Poppa's kitchen. That was his special knock, a morse code "B" for Bertram. He had to repeat this ritual four times until Poppa finally opened the door.

"Did you start without me?" Bertram asked anxiously.

"Of course not. I was only setting up," Poppa replied.

He led Bertram through the small kitchen into a wide hall, off of which opened doors leading to a bedroom, a bathroom and a library. The last door brought them into the living room, and from there, they entered the lab through another door much like the one connecting Poppa's apartment to the storage area.

"Have some candy." Poppa offered Bertram a glass jar filled with chocolate and bonbons.

"No, thanks. I'm too excited to eat. Tonight's the night!"

Poppa shrugged his bony shoulders. "We'll see," he said. The first thing Bertram saw was the massive lab table, covered with several tubes, some strangely shaped glassware, and jars and bottles of various secret ingredients. At one end stood a large pot, which looked suspiciously like a caldron.

"What I still don't understand," Bertram said, "is if you mix all that stuff together, why do you have to pour it through all that plastic and glass?"

"The ancient Egyptians developed the formula, but it didn't always work. I thought if we filtered it, we'd make it more pure — and thus, more effective."

Bertram watched as Poppa measured a large assortment of powders and liquids and added

8

them to the pot. Then he turned a light on underneath. Immediately he smelled a disgusting odor, which was followed by a faint trail of smoke.

"Woof! You'd better shut off the smoke detector for this one," Poppa said. "Otherwise the sprinkler system will go off and rain on my parade."

"What do we call this stuff when it's done?" Bertram asked.

"Well, the Egyptians called it by a name that translates to 'that which makes the unalive walk.' What a mouthful! How about if we just call it X-13, for today's date, October 13?"

"Fine with me," Bertram said. "How long does this stuff take?"

"Oh, not more than about twenty minutes."

Bertram was shocked. "Just twenty minutes for a formula that might change the whole face of the world?" he asked.

"Well, it has to cool for a little while," Poppa said.

"And then how long will it take to work?"

"How am I supposed to know? The Egyptians didn't leave us *that* much information."

"Could it take all night?" Bertram persisted.

"It's possible."

"Then it's a good thing tomorrow's Saturday. But what if the statue starts to walk when the Fear Factory is full of people on tours?"

"Then your father will probably charge extra on the way out!" Poppa said.

Bertram laughed and then settled in to watch the creation of formula X-13.

An hour later, he and Poppa were making their way through the Hall of Monsters, the least scary area of the museum. Poppa was carrying the jar of distilled formula, on top of which was a device that looked a little like an oil can. Bertram carried two paintbrushes to spread the liquid around once it had been squirted on the figures.

"What do you say, shall we start with Frankenstein's monster and his bride?" Poppa asked.

"Okay," Bertram agreed.

Poppa grinned as he squeezed a few drops of the X-13 onto the monster's head. Bertram worked quickly to spread it. The monster already looked so lifelike that Bertram half expected it to giggle when he brushed the liquid under its arms. Then they applied the formula to Frankenstein's bride.

Their tasks complete, Poppa and Bertram sat back with the half-empty jar of X-13 and waited to see what would happen.

— Two —

When seven o'clock came, Poppa said, "It doesn't look like anything's going to happen. You'd better go upstairs and pretend that you slept in your room all night. I'll stay here another half hour, in case our friend decides to wake up."

"Poppa, what if the monster or his bride start moving around while the tourists are here?" Bertram asked nervously.

"What are you worried about? It will be splendid. The tourists will love it!" Poppa paused and said more quietly, "I doubt that will happen. It's too bad that I can't figure out what went wrong with the formula."

"Are you sure we were supposed to brush it on?" Bertram asked.

"Of course. How else?" Poppa said. "They didn't have electric paint sprayers in ancient Egypt."

"Just one more question before I go," Bertram said. "Say we get the statue to move. What will it do? And how do we get it to stop walking around?"

"That's two questions," said Poppa. "Don't worry, I'll keep an eye on our friend. Now, run along, or you'll be doing all your worrying in your room for the next month."

A few minutes later, Bertram slipped into his room with just enough time to take a shower and change clothes before breakfast. The hot water felt good on his back and legs, which were a little stiff from sleeping curled up on the floor and leaning against the wall. As the steam swirled around him, he thought about the X-13 and why it hadn't worked. He didn't want to admit that it might just be another one of Poppa's harebrained schemes, like the invisible cloak and the vampire vaccine.

"Good morning!" Dora sang to Bertram as he entered the kitchen.

His parents came in right behind him. Even though it was Saturday, his father was wearing a white shirt and tie.

"How do the September figures look, Clark?" his mother asked, sipping her black coffee. Bertram's parents staged financial discussions at meals for his benefit. Bertram called it "The Clark and Marie Show."

Mr. Potter slowly chewed a piece of bacon, then answered, "Receipts are up twelve percent over the same month last year, but expenses are up nine. Mostly utilities. Year to end of the third quarter is up ten percent against the same nine percent expenses. So it looks like we're running one percent ahead of last year."

Mrs. Potter put some syrup on her plate. "That's almost as flat as this pancake," she said, pointing at it with her fork. "But it's not bad, since we actually made a nice profit last year. I guess we'll do it again."

"If that new exhibit my father is working on ever gets finished, it should help," Bertram's father said in between bites of pancake. "Especially over Thanksgiving and Christmas."

Bertram had been listening without saying a word. He always pretended he didn't know "The Clark and Marie Show" was directed at him. "Well, I guess I'll be going, if I'm excused," he said, and he brought his dishes over to the sink.

"No seconds today?" Dora asked.

"Got work to do," Bertram said breezily.

As he hurried downstairs, he thought he heard his father say, "Well, at least the boy shows responsibility."

Bertram strutted into the bright front lobby of the Fear Factory, the only part of the museum beside the gift shop that had windows. He took a feather duster from a storage cabinet and began to dust off the racks of tourist brochures and monster-related information that they displayed. Then he unlocked the gift shop,

14

dusted around in there, and opened up the ticket window.

Bertram took tickets on Saturday mornings from ten o'clock, when the Fear Factory opened, until lunchtime. His mother took over after lunch. That way, they saved a whole day's salary. On Sunday, although the Factory was open only from noon to five, no one from the family worked. They needed a day off!

Dusting and whistling, Bertram almost forgot about the night before. When he remembered, he hurriedly put away the duster and pushed open the heavy metal door to the Hall of Monsters.

Flipping on the light switch, Bertram ran down the twisting corridor until he came to a dead stop in front of the Frankenstein's monster exhibit. There stood the creatures, as lifeless as the day Poppa had made them. Bertram's heart sank. He shuffled the rest of the way to Poppa's apartment.

His knock was answered almost instantly by his grinning grandfather.

"What are you so happy about?" Bertram snapped, unable to hide his disappointment.

"It looks like you got up on the wrong side of the floor this morning," Poppa said.

"Don't you even care that the X-13 didn't work?" Bertram asked.

15

"Of course I care," Poppa answered. "But I'm not going to let it ruin my day. Maybe it just takes a while."

Bertram shook his head. "Well, see you later," he said abruptly, then hurried back along the dim halls toward the front desk.

It was time to open, and a short line had already formed outside. Bertram smiled as he threw open the massive front door. "Welcome to the Fear Factory!" he announced cheerfully. "Be prepared to be scared!"

After his shift at the ticket window, Bertram decided to spend the rest of the day hanging around the museum. He pretended to be a visitor, and joined a group of tourists as they passed through the door into the Hall of Monsters. Sometimes he liked to pretend he was seeing the exhibits for the first time. Other times he tried to look for tiny details that might have escaped him. Mostly he liked to eavesdrop on the visitors, watching their reactions and listening to their comments.

The Fear Factory was really a wonderful place, and it drew a wide range of comments. Some people liked its narrow, twisting corridors. Others hated them. The same could be said for the small, intimately horrifying dioramas; the larger displays under soaring ceilings with nasty things hanging down from them;

the random wax monster lurking in a dark corner; the sudden figure lunging out. And then there was the creepy music and the grisly narration.

Although the Hall of Monsters was ghastly enough for some visitors, it was generally agreed to be the tamest of the Fear Factory's three main sections. The Rooms of Blood ran from the slightly more horrific to the spectacularly blood-chilling.

But the Chambers of Doom, with their carefully engineered special effects, were for only the strongest of heart and stomach. In fact, the Potters actually kept a registered nurse on staff in case there were any casualties among the tourists. To date, however, fainting had been the worst reaction.

Bertram decided he would not look ahead to the Frankenstein monster display, but rather let it take him by surprise. He took his place between an elderly couple and a young family with three kids.

He wondered how long the kids would last before their parents would have to carry them, screaming, out of the waxworks. When he was at the window, he always warned people personally that it was strong stuff and gave them a chance not to go in.

His father frowned on the practice. He said that people could read the warning signs, and if they insisted on taking young children into the exhibits, they had to accept the consequences.

"Look at that, Helen," the elderly man said. "There's that scene out of *Dracula* that always reminded me of you."

"Oh, George," his wife said. "Go on."

As the little group moved to the next exhibit, the oldest of the children, who looked no more than six, said in a loud voice, "Daddy, what's that button?"

Bertram was about to answer when the boy went ahead and pushed it. The area, which had been almost completely dark, began to get faintly brighter. The setting looked very much like the bayou behind the Fear Factory. In fact, Poppa and Sigmund had copied many of the effects from it. There were trees overgrown with vines and water plants, and a thick fog covered the marshy ground.

Bertram held his breath; he knew what was coming. An arm, covered with weeds and moss, slowly began to reach out of the swamp. It could easily take somebody by surprise because it blended in so well with the surroundings. Suddenly, the creature to which the arm was attached lunged upward out of the swamp, and grasped toward the audience.

The children started screaming, but when the creature slunk back into the swamp and they slowly realized there was a plate of glass separating it from them, they calmed down and even let out a few giggles. But the oldest kid, the boy who had pushed the button that started the whole exhibit, could not stop shrieking. Finally, the father told them they would all have to leave if he couldn't be quiet. The boy immediately closed his mouth, and the family moved on to the next exhibit.

When they went into the next room, Bertram decided to stay behind. He wanted to watch a larger group's reaction to the swamp creature, and a dozen teenagers had just entered the room. When no one noticed the button, Bertram decided to push it himself. They hardly paid any attention to the arm as it climbed out of the black water. Suddenly one of the girls, whose back had been to the display, turned around and came face to face with the creature. She let out a little high-pitched yelp, then she whooped with hysterical laughter.

"Looks like your cousin Fred," one girl said to the boy standing next to her.

"Fred's uglier," the boy answered.

"This place is a joke," another boy commented. "Is this supposed to be scary?"

"It's probably scary if you're a two-year-old," said another.

Bertram couldn't stand it when people — especially obnoxious jerks — badmouthed the

Fear Factory. If they wanted to be really frightened, he knew just how to do it. They would be sorry they ever set foot in his family's museum.

Running through the hallways, Bertram finally came to the hidden stairway known only to the residents and staff of the Factory. These took him to a small landing on the second floor from which a door opened into the Costume Room. Bertram quickly made his selection, put it on, and hurried back downstairs, making sure he wasn't seen. Then with his passkey he let himself into section three of the Chambers of Doom.

Making sure it was empty, he shuffled across the viewing area and climbed onto the low stage. He crouched in the corner and waited. Several groups came and went, activating the scene of "Werewolf in the Girls' Dormitory" by their entrance through the regular door. Bertram grew impatient. He couldn't see his watch, but he figured that nearly an hour had passed. He couldn't imagine that the teens had chickened out somewhere along the way.

Finally he heard the door open, and in the dim light he recognized them. He licked his lips with glee. He heard one girl say, "I'm tired of standing around in all these dark rooms. Let's go."

Another girl answered, "You're just scared."

"Yeah?" said the first. "Who's been hollering for her mommy ever since we came in?"

The bickering stopped as the scene began to get brighter. The group actually stood there without saying anything as the four very life-like girls went about making preparations for bedtime, unaware that the werewolf was climbing though the window into their room. When the first of them turned around, taped screams echoed in the room. Then the werewolf actually attacked the girl while her roommates looked on in grisly horror.

That was Bertram's cue. When he came out from the wings, one of the boys noticed him. "Hey, what's that?" he said, surprised.

"It's just another werewolf," said another.

"Yeah, but where did it come from?" said the first.

By this time, all eyes were on Bertram.

Instead of stopping at the front of the stage, he continued to walk right off it, toward the two girls who had been talking earlier.

"This isn't any wax statue," said one of the girls. "This is real!" she shrieked.

If any of the kids had stopped to think, they would have realized they weren't in any danger. But once they started pushing and screaming, the rest of them weren't willing to stand around dealing with their friends and the werewolf. So they all wound up piling through the emergency exit as fast as they could push each other.

Bertram laughed all the way back to the Costume Room.

That evening, when Poppa came up for dinner, Bertram pulled him aside. "One of the exhibits came to life today," he whispered.

"No! Tell me," Poppa pleaded.

"Well, it wasn't Frankenstein's monster," Bertram replied, sorry to disappoint his grandfather. "It was the werewolf." He explained the afternoon's incident.

"Very funny, Bertram. I wish we could be as successful with the other statues," Poppa said. "But it's not over yet."

"I'll tell you what's not over yet," Bertram's mother said, coming into the dining room. "This!" She was waving a flier that had been photocopied onto bright yellow paper.

Bertram took the flier from his mother. It read:

HORACE Q. WRIGHT, MAYOR OF BLACK BAYOU, RE-QUESTS THE HONOR OF YOUR PRESENCE AT A MEETING OF THE TOWN OF BLACK BAYOU ON THURSDAY, OCTOBER 18, AT 8:00 P.M. MEMBERS OF THE CITIZENS FOR DECENCY, OF WHICH YOUR MAYOR IS CHAIRMAN, WILL PRESENT A LIST OF REASONS WHY THE FEAR FACTORY, THAT SITE OF CORRUPTION IN OUR FAIR TOWN, OUGHT TO CLOSE ITS DOORS FOREVER. PROTECT THE YOUTH OF OUR TOWN!

COME OUT TO THE MEETING AND VOTE TO CLOSE
THE FEAR FACTORY!

"The nerve!" she shouted, her face flushing.

"Now, Marie," Bertram's father said, coming up behind her, "they've tried stuff like this before, and they've never gotten anywhere with it."

"But that was before Horace Q. Wright became mayor," Bertram's mother reminded him.

"He thinks that just because the people of this town lost their heads temporarily and elected him mayor, they'll let him close their biggest tourist attraction. But the folks who depend on our business for their business will never vote against us. They'll lose too much money. Don't worry."

"Don't worry? That's what you always say, Clark. Well, I'm plenty worried," Mrs. Potter said angrily. "But if Horace Q. Wright thinks we'll close up without a fight, he has another thing coming!"

— Three —

The week did not start out well for Bertram. Aside from trying to puzzle out why the X-13 didn't work, now he had to worry about the Fear Factory closing and losing his home.

On Sunday night, Bertram couldn't sleep. It was well after midnight when he trudged through the deserted corridors of the museum, flashlight in hand, to see if Poppa was still awake.

He had heard that the older you get, the less sleep you need. Poppa often could get along on three hours' sleep for weeks on end. But then, Poppa wasn't normal in any way.

Outside Poppa's apartment, Bertram heard faint music coming through the door. It sounded like an old musical was on television, one of those big extravaganzas from the thirties that Poppa loved. Poppa always said that putting one of those movies together seemed like magic to him.

Bertram knocked four times, and Poppa opened the door.

"Hello, Bertram," Poppa said warmly. "I'm delighted to see you, but you'll be in a barrel of trouble if your parents know I let you in at this hour."

"I couldn't sleep," Bertram complained. "I'm too worried."

"Nonsense," Poppa said. "What's the use of worrying? It doesn't do any good. If I ever feel like worrying, I watch an old movie or mix up something I like to eat. If something bad is going to happen, I might as well not give myself a hard time in advance." He smiled.

Bertram wasn't convinced. "I guess I'll be going now," he said. "Thanks for the advice." He dearly loved Poppa, but in a crisis, his grandfather wasn't very comforting. The man not only refused to worry, but he didn't seem to understand the concept.

The next day at school Bertram was exhausted. "What's with you today?" Wesley asked at snack time. "You look like you just climbed out of the mummy's tomb."

"I-I'm just tired," Bertram answered absent-mindedly, biting off a piece of graham cracker with peanut butter and marshmallow cream on it. "I didn't get much sleep last night."

"How come? Up late working on something for the museum?"

"No, I was just worried. Did you see the flier from Horace Q. Wright about closing down the Fear Factory?"

"Oh, that," Wesley said, stuffing a carrot stick into his mouth. "You can't take a lunatic like that too seriously."

"The town elected him mayor, didn't it?" Bertram asked.

Wesley swallowed before answering, "If Wright closes you down, I promise to organize all the kids in town to go on strike until you can open up again."

"That's great!" Bertram said wholeheartedly. "But you've never even organized a baseball game, Wesley. How are you going to get the whole town together?"

"I'd tell my parents, and they'd tell all their friends. My father knows lots of people through his real estate business. You'll see."

"Thanks," Bertram said, feeling a little better. "The other thing I'm worried about is this formula my grandfather made that can bring a statue to life. It hasn't worked yet."

"How do you know it can bring a statue to life if it hasn't worked?" Wesley asked, pushing the bridge of his glasses up on his nose.

"It isn't his invention," Bertram answered. "He was just following an ancient Egyptian formula."

"Sometimes you're really gullible," Wesley said.

"Really what?" Bertram asked.

"Easy to put one over on."

Just then the bell rang, signaling the end of snack time.

"See you after school?" Wesley asked hopefully.

"I guess so," Bertram mumbled.

When Bertram and Wesley reached Bertram's house after school, Dora was just taking a fresh batch of brownies out of the oven. "Now, don't touch those," she warned. "They're steaming hot. Wait until they cool some." Then she disappeared downstairs.

"What do you want to do until the brownies are ready?" Bertram asked Wesley.

"Have any new comics?"

"None you haven't seen already. But you gave me an idea. I want to try to figure out why that X-13 didn't work. I thought maybe we could go through my comic books and find stories about mummies coming to life, and maybe I'll get an idea."

"You really are naive," Wesley said, pushing his glasses up. "Your grandfather probably mixed up a formula for muscle ointment or something. I can't blame you for liking him, but you've got to admit he's a crazy old man."

27

"Take that back, Wesley Fairchild!" Bertram demanded.

"I won't. It's true."

"Take that back, or I'm going to punch you right on your stupid little nose, if I can find it underneath those goggles you wear!"

"You take that back!" Wesley screamed, his face becoming redder by the moment, which looked strange against his white-blond hair.

"Not until you take back what you said about my grandfather."

"Never!" Wesley cried.

"Then prepare to defend yourself," Bertram threatened.

"Wait. I have to take my glasses off."

"But how will you see without them?" Bertram asked. Even though he was mad, he didn't want to hit a guy who couldn't see the punch coming.

"I can't," Wesley conceded. "But if they get broken, my mother will kill me. I've already broken three pairs this year."

"Suit yourself," Bertram said. "But get ready. Here I come."

Wesley placed his thick glasses on the dining room table, and swung out at Bertram without warning. Bertram easily jumped out of his arm's reach and danced around Wesley, who could barely keep up with him.

"You'd think by now you would have developed your own sonar," Bertram taunted.

"That's radar," Wesley said. "And besides, I can see. Just not without my glasses."

Bertram, meanwhile, sneaked behind Wesley's back and got his head in a hammerhold. "Now, take back what you said about my grandfather, or you're history," Bertram said loudly right into Wesley's ear.

"No! You're as crazy as he is. Get me out of here. Help!"

Dora, who was just coming upstairs, heard Wesley's scream and came to his rescue. But Bertram wouldn't let go. "I've never seen you two like this before!" she said.

"He insulted Poppa!" Bertram said breathlessly as Wesley elbowed him in the stomach. "He called Poppa a crazy old man."

"That's because he is. Everybody knows that," Wesley croaked as Bertram's grip grew tighter.

"Now, you two stop that right now, or I'll have to do something drastic!" Dora scolded. But neither boy would give in.

Dora quickly got between the two boys and forced them apart. "Now, you two wrestling stars come in here and sit down. Have some milk and brownies and just cool off. And tell me what this is all about."

Bertram quickly told her about their argument, still hurt by Wesley's accusations.

Dora shook her head and laughed. "Now, Bertram," she said, "everybody *knows* your Poppa is a crazy old man. But that's why we love him."

"Mom and Dad don't love him," he said, dismayed that Dora was taking Wesley's side.

"If they'd get up from behind those account books of theirs long enough to take a good look, they would. Which means they really do. And I'm sure Wesley does, too."

Bertram looked at his friend, whose face was still watermelon pink. He wasn't so sure. Wesley just sat there eating a brownie.

Dora bustled around in the refrigerator, pulling out a number of ingredients and putting them on the counter. It was clear that no one wanted to talk, so Bertram watched as Dora mixed the ingredients together and got them ready to put into a casserole dish.

Just then an idea came to him — an idea so simple and yet so brilliant, that he could hardly keep from jumping out of his seat. He decided, however, to hide his excitement the best he could — especially from Wesley.

"Crazy old man" indeed. He'd show Wesley — and Dora, too!

The next day after school Bertram ran home and went straight to Poppa's lab. "Bertram, what a nice surprise!" Poppa said. "You're just in time to watch us pour our new statue. Presenting . . . The Man Being Boiled Alive!"

Bertram looked over at the mold his grandfather had made. Even without the wax poured in, he could tell the new figure would be absolutely horrifying.

"This will take the place of the mummy exhibit until I can build a new one that gives the tourists more to see. For example, an actual mummy being prepared, or one coming back from the dead." Poppa grinned, then licked his lips excitedly.

"Uh, where's Sigmund?" Bertram asked, not seeing his grandfather's assistant in the room.

"He had to do a little business," Poppa replied. "Come, take off your jacket and sit down," Poppa said. "When Sigmund comes back, we'll be just about ready to pour."

Poppa went to check on the huge vat of liquid boiling away on the enormous laboratory stove. The stove was set close to the floor so that he could inspect the large pots without having to climb up onto a ladder.

Bertram scanned the shelves until his eyes fell on the remaining X-13, which Poppa had stored in a bottle. Just then a little light went on next to the stove. It was the signal Poppa

32

had rigged up to let him know the tea kettle was screeching in the kitchen. Poppa refused to allow food preparation in the lab.

"Ah!" said Poppa. "Just in time. I'll go fix the tea while Siggy is still busy." With that, he turned and left the lab.

Bertram never did anything that affected the waxworks without first checking with Poppa. But this time he had to. He was convinced that he was doing the right thing, no matter how risky.

Without losing a moment, he hopped off his stool, grabbed the X-13 off the shelf and poured some into the boiling wax.

—— **Four** ——

Bertram had just enough time to replace the missing formula with an equal amount of water before Poppa returned to the lab with his tea. "Are you staying to watch us pour the wax?" Poppa asked Bertram.

"Uh, no, I was just thinking, in fact, that I'd better be getting upstairs. I've got some English homework to do, and my parents will be wondering where I am."

"Well, you'll miss a great pouring," Poppa said. "That is, if Siggy ever gets back. Where is he?"

Bertram left before the assistant could return. He raced up the stairs, into his room, and flopped on the bed, pulling the pillow over his head to muffle his whoops of triumph. Now the hard part was here — the wait. Bertram was so excited that he couldn't believe his plan wouldn't work.

That night, when Poppa came up to dinner, it was all Bertram could do to keep from telling him what he had done.

34

As he was passing the fried chicken, Bertram's father asked Poppa, "Did you get that new figure poured today — what's it called, The Man Being Fried to Death?"

Bertram choked at the mention of the name.

"The Man Being Boiled Alive," Poppa corrected his son.

"Whatever," Mr. Potter said. "Pretty gruesome sight, I imagine, whatever it is."

"You'll have to see it for yourself. It's my masterpiece, if I do say so myself," said Poppa, transferring a chicken leg from the serving plate to his own.

"Where's Sigmund, your partner in crime?" Mrs. Potter asked.

"He's not feeling too well tonight. I just made him some tea and toast," Poppa said.

"He didn't get sick from looking at the statue, did he?" Bertram's father said, putting a biscuit on his plate.

"No, not him," said Poppa. "He has a cast-iron stomach."

"Well, tell him I hope he feels better real soon so he can pour more masterpieces," Mr. Potter replied, slipping a square of cornbread onto his plate. "Yuck, stewed tomatoes."

"I heard that," Dora said as she came through the doorway, carrying a bowl of green beans. "You don't know what good is."

"Maybe so," Mr. Potter said, "but I know what I like, and it isn't stewed tomatoes.

"What kind of example is that to set for the boy?" Dora asked with mock seriousness.

"I'd say it's not such a bad one, compared to some *other* examples he sees around here," Mr. Potter said, staring at his father.

Changing the subject quickly, Mrs. Potter asked, "When will the new statue be cool, Poppa? And how soon can you get the display ready?"

"The display *is* all ready," said Poppa, a trifle annoyed. "And the statue will be cooled by morning."

And gone, if the X-13 worked, Bertram thought to himself.

The next afternoon, when Bertram arrived home from school, he went right to the storeroom. That was where Poppa and Sigmund had taken The Man Being Boiled Alive until they were ready to place him in his scene. The display was wonderful. It consisted of an oversized see-through vat and an evil, gleeful-looking "chef" crouching on a catwalk above, pushing at the hapless victim's head with a huge cooking spoon as if it were a dumpling.

Bertram had seen all the sketches and plans for The Man Being Boiled Alive, but not even he was ready for the hideousness of the new

36

figure. When he came upon it in the storeroom, it made him jump.

Poppa had outdone himself. The man was so realistic! The scald marks on the face and wrinkled skin on the body — twisted in agony — made the figure especially grotesque.

For a minute Bertram wondered if Horace Q. Wright was correct in believing that the Fear Factory corrupted young people. But Poppa had explained to him that the museum didn't create evil — it merely depicted it. On other occasions, he had heard people say that the Factory was just giving people what they wanted and doing it better than any other museum.

Deep down, Bertram didn't believe his family was depraved, but sometimes he wondered about some of the rituals and the interest in magic he shared with Poppa. As Bertram stood beside The Man Being Boiled Alive, he wondered if he was only kidding himself about the X-13 actually working. Maybe Poppa *was* just a crazy old man. The statue certainly didn't look as if it was about to go anywhere.

Bertram checked on the new statue throughout the afternoon, but each time it was as lifeless as before. When he went down to check on it just before dinner, a scary thought occurred to him: If the X-13 really worked on The Man Being Boiled Alive, what would the statue *do*?

Bertram had no idea — but as frightening as it could be, he wanted to find out. He dashed back upstairs and took a seat at the dinner table next to Poppa just as his parents walked into the room. Dora placed a huge tureen of gumbo on the table, followed by an enormous loaf of French bread.

"I thought we'd have a quick dinner tonight," Bertram's mother explained. "We want to get to the town meeting early so that we can get seats right in front. Horace Q. Wright will undoubtedly stock the place with his Citizens for Decency, and they'll hog the good seats. I've called all my friends, and they promised to be there. Ida Mae Latour said she would bring her bridge club, too. And your father has gotten the support of some of the influential chamber of commerce members," she informed Bertram.

Whenever Mrs. Potter got excited, she began to talk very fast, and this night was no exception. Suddenly she jumped up and started to dish out the gumbo herself — apparently Dora wasn't moving fast enough for her.

"What's gotten into you, Marie?" Bertram's father asked. "We still have two hours till the meeting starts."

"It will take us at least fifteen minutes to eat, and fifteen minutes to get there and park, so that leaves only an hour and a half," she replied between mouthfuls.

"Well, I won't have my digestion ruined because of this meeting," Mr. Potter said defiantly.

"You'd better place this meeting ahead of your digestion," his wife retorted, "because if we don't fight this thing through, you won't have anything *to* digest."

"Well, I've already finished my homework," Bertram announced, "so I'm all set to go to the meeting."

"Nothing doing," his mother said firmly. "That meeting is no place for a young boy. It might get ugly."

"But Mom, it's my home, too. And someday, the Fear Factory will belong to me."

"He's right, Marie. Let the boy go," Poppa said quietly.

"Not only is Bertram not going," Bertram's mother replied, "but neither are you!"

"I'm not going?" Poppa asked, confused.

"No, you're not. Clark and I decided that you'd only hurt our case. You know that when you get started, you tell every last little detail of every last little escapade around here, whether they're true or not. Some of your little stories might frighten our neighbors even more. No, I'm afraid that Clark and Dora and I will represent this family. I hope you understand. Our lawyer advised us to present the Fear Factory as an upstanding enterprise. And

39

that means no silly stories about magic potions and talking cats and that sort of thing.

"Besides," Marie continued, hardly pausing for breath, "isn't tonight the full moon? Don't you and Bertram always plan some kind of mischief every full moon? You'll have plenty to keep you busy without coming to the meeting," she concluded.

Bertram knew that Poppa hated to be talked to like a child. At the moment, he was quieter than Bertram had ever seen him. The elderly man quietly rose from the table, wiped his mouth, folded the napkin and placed it on his chair, then left the room.

Bertram followed and tried to talk to Poppa, but his grandfather just waved his grandson away. "I'll be all right," Poppa said. "Just give me a little time."

For his part, Bertram was sad that his parents felt that way about Poppa — almost ashamed of him, it seemed. But then he tried to imagine himself representing the Fear Factory in court. Would he want to have Poppa as a witness? Probably not, he had to admit.

But Bertram didn't see why *he* couldn't go to the meeting. He was allowed to go to soccer games, where the crowd got as rowdy as this one was likely to. He went upstairs to his room to sulk.

During the next few minutes, he heard doors opening and shutting as his parents and Dora got ready to go. Finally, stealing into his parents' dark office, he looked out the window and saw their car disappear down the road.

Bertram paced in his room, which wasn't easy since there was very little unoccupied floor space. In addition to his bed, there was a huge horsehair sofa that he had insisted on having when his mother had bought a new couch. There was his desk, an old rolltop model he'd rescued from his parents' office. And there were the bookshelves and display cases that held his huge comic book collection along with some model planes, toy monsters, and horror movie mementoes.

Bertram picked up, and then threw down, several books. He definitely didn't feel like reading. Pacing some more, he looked at his walls, plastered with horror movie posters. Then he decided to pay another visit to The Man Being Boiled Alive. He opened his door and headed downstairs.

Flipping on the light in the storage area, Bertram decided that the room wasn't as creepy as he had thought it was a couple of years ago. Immediately his glance flew over to the corner where the statue was — or, rather, where the statue had been. It was gone! Completely, utterly gone!

"I can't believe it!" Bertram cried. "The formula worked!"

Suddenly Bertram was filled with a mixture of glee and dread. What if the statue really had moved on its own? What if the statue had escaped from the museum — on the same night as the town meeting?

If The Man Being Boiled Alive was seen in public, the town would close down the Fear Factory for sure!

— Five —

Bertram ran to Poppa's apartment as fast as he could, banging into walls on the way. He was in too much of a hurry to use his flashlight or turn on the lights. Without bothering to use the special code, he pounded several times on the door.

"All right, I'm coming, I'm coming," he heard his grandfather's voice call.

When the door opened, Bertram blurted out, "Tell me you didn't move it!"

"Tell you I didn't move what?" Poppa said.

"It's gone!" Bertram shouted.

"What's gone?"

"It — the statue — The Man Being Boiled Alive!" Bertram cried.

"Impossible!" Poppa said. "I'll go look myself."

"Do you think Siggy could have moved it?" Bertram asked while tugging on Poppa's sleeve as they hurried back toward the storage room.

"No," Poppa said. "Siggy never does anything unless I tell him it's okay. Besides, he hasn't been feeling very well lately, as you know. He couldn't possibly have moved it himself."

"Then there are only two possibilities," Bertram said boldly. "Either somebody broke in here and stole the statue, or. . . . " He couldn't bring himself to confess to what he had done.

"Or what?" Poppa asked, sounding impatient.

"Or . . .I-I don't know," Bertram stammered.

"Well, just for the record, let's pay a call on Siggy," Poppa announced.

Bertram nearly had to run to keep up with his grandfather's long strides through the Fear Factory to a little-used corridor behind the Hall of Monsters. He knocked at the door to the room where his assistant lived.

They could hear the buzz of Sigmund's TV in the background. Like Bertram's parents, Siggy was addicted to old shows on cable.

Poppa knocked again, more forcefully.

The door opened a crack, and Sigmund peered out at them. "Vat you vant?" he said through the crack. That was Siggy — always the charming host.

"Siggy, come out. We have to talk to you!" Poppa said in a businesslike tone that Bertram rarely heard him use.

The door opened just wide enough to let the little man into the hallway. Sigmund was about six inches shorter than Bertram, but with his big head, large piercing eyes and mop of thick black hair, he had a certain larger-than-life appearance. After having spent three days in bed with a cold, his hair looked even wilder than usual.

"So talk," Siggy urged.

"My masterpiece is missing!" Poppa cried.

"Missing? How? Somevone stole it?" Sigmund asked, his eyes wide with surprise.

"That's what we don't know."

"So vy you come to me? I don't know nutting."

"There's only one other explanation," Bertram said, feeling bolder all of a sudden. "The X-13 must have worked."

"What?" said Poppa.

"The X-13," Bertram repeated. "You must have gotten the formula right after all. Maybe all it needed was time."

"What are you talking about?" Poppa replied. "I didn't use any X-13 in The Man Being Boiled Alive."

"No, but I did," Bertram said with a sense of triumph. "While you were making tea, I slipped some into the mixture. I had faith in you, and I knew we just had to give it another chance to work."

"This is awful!" Poppa exclaimed.

"I know," Bertram agreed. "Especially on the night of the town meeting. If the statue has left the building, who knows what it'll do."

"No, that part isn't awful. What's awful is that we weren't around to see the statue come to life!" Poppa said vehemently.

Poppa took one look at Sigmund, and the two locked arms and began dancing in a little circle while singing some long-forgotten song in two distinctly different keys.

When Bertram was finally able to break in, he said, "Look, I'm as excited as you are about all this. But we have to search this place and find out where the statue went." Poppa and Sigmund finally stopped dancing and the three of them split up to search the museum, deciding to meet back at the lab.

"Well," Bertram said when they had gathered in the lab half an hour later. "We've searched every corner of this place and he's not here. We've got to go out looking for him."

"I think I know where you'd like us to start," Poppa said. "At that meeting. If I get your point, it could be a little embarrassing for your parents if "The Man" shows up."

"Do you know what to do if we catch him?" Bertram asked. "Do you know how to undo the effects of the X-13?"

"Not really," Poppa admitted. "But I doubt he'll be violent. We should be able to bring him in peacefully."

"But what will my parents say when they see us at the meeting?" Bertram asked.

"They're not going to see us," Poppa said with a twinkle in his eyes. "This is one circumstance in which living at the Fear Factory has its advantages!"

He quickly led them up to the Costume Room, where Poppa took about thirty years off his age with the proper makeup and clothes, while Bertram dressed as an old man, with a wig and a cane to complete his ensemble. "And you," Poppa said to Sigmund, who stood and watched them dress up, "will wait outside and serve as our getaway car. Now, let's go!" he said excitedly.

"There's just one problem," Bertram said. "Your driver's license."

"What about it?" said Poppa earnestly.

"You don't have one, remember? The police took it away last time. They said you were a menace on the roads."

"Well, you know I'm not a menace. Just because I took a shortcut across the park, they took my license away. I don't get it. I stayed on the paths!" Poppa insisted.

"Look, Poppa, I know you were careful, but that doesn't matter now. If anything happens while you're driving, it would be awful. We're in enough trouble with this town already. Let's ride the bus or walk."

"But that will take too long," Poppa argued.

Bertram crossed his arms over his chest. "Well, I'm not going if you drive."

"All right, then, Sigmund will drive," Poppa announced.

Siggy looked startled. "Who, me?" he asked.

"Yes. You're an excellent driver once we get enough pillows on the seat to bring you up high enough to see over the steering wheel."

Siggy shrugged. "Vell, if I must." They went outside and he headed toward the Fear Factory van.

"No, not that," Poppa instructed him. "They'll know it's us. We'll take the old convertible."

"Poppa, they'll know it's us in that, too. Who else in town has a 1957 black convertible with a fat white stripe down the side?"

"In mint condition, too," Poppa said proudly.

Bertram thought a minute, then shrugged and said, "Oh, I guess you're right. At least it's your car. If you cracked up the van, you'd really get it."

"Such confidence in his grandfather this young boy has!" Poppa said with a chuckle. He ducked back inside the building and came back with three sturdy cushions. "These should

48

make you more comfortable," he said to Siggy, handing him the car keys, as well.

Then the three of them went around to a large garage that stood at the end of the driveway, about a hundred yards behind the Fear Factory. They climbed into the car and Siggy started the engine with a roar.

"We're off!" Bertram shouted from the back seat.

"Now, go down Lafayette to Marquette and up Trey and then hang a right at Fortune . . . " Poppa loved to give drivers directions. It irritated Bertram's father to no end.

But Sigmund didn't seem to mind Poppa's help, and they arrived at the courthouse without a hitch. "Now, you stay in the car and wait for us because we might need to make a quick getaway. And don't go to sleep," Poppa warned Siggy.

Then he and Bertram climbed out of the car and made their way across the parking lot. It was just after eight o'clock, and no one else was outside. Bertram and Poppa entered the building unnoticed and slipped into the courtroom.

The room was packed, and noisy. Horace Q. Wright was seated at the judge's bench. He was trying to call the meeting to order by banging a gavel, but no one was paying any attention to him.

49

On the right side of the room, in the jury box, sat the Citizens for Decency group. They were all wearing white buttons and white caps with a red "C" and a navy blue "D" on them. Mr. and Mrs. Potter, Dora and several of their friends were sitting in the front row, on the left side of the courtroom.

One of the CDers, as they were known, a tall woman with red hair, was shouting something at Bertram's parents that he couldn't quite make out. Bertram's father said something back to the woman, and she blushed. Then the two of them started to scream at each other.

Poppa and Bertram found aisle seats in the back row near the door, which gave them a fairly good view and an easy exit. The noise got louder as more people joined the shouting match. Bertram half-expected someone to start throwing tomatoes.

Instead, he saw Horace pull out a small gun and aim it at the ceiling. A shot rang out, and the ruckus stopped immediately.

"Don't worry, folks," Horace said good-naturedly. "It was only a blank. But we've got to call this meeting to order and get down to business. Now, as you all know, we're here to-night to hear both sides on this Fear Factory issue. On my left" — he pointed to the jury box with his gavel — "I have an outstanding group of this town's citizens, who propose to shut

50

down that den of horror. And over here," he said, motioning to the Potters, "are the owners of said sinful establishment and all of its evil creatures."

"I wonder whose side he's on," the woman next to Bertram said sarcastically. "I don't think it's possible for those people to get a fair hearing with him in charge."

Bertram nodded, then focused his attention on the proceedings. Horace called the red-haired lady from the Citizens of Decency to the witness stand. "Don't I need to place my hand on the Bible first, Horace?" she asked.

"No, Mary Lou. This isn't a trial. It's only a hearing."

Mary Lou pursed her lips. "Well, all right. But I promise I'm telling the whole truth anyway."

Several people in the audience giggled.

Horace smiled politely. "Now, Mary Lou, why don't you tell the folks here about your visit to the Fear Factory."

Mary Lou glanced over at her fellow CDers. "You all know I would never set foot inside such a despicable place! But I felt it was my civic duty to see what's destroying our town. So last Thursday I went and had a look. Why, I declare I have never seen such depravity in my entire life. The filth, the horror, the violence,

51

that was shown in that there — I won't glorify it by calling it a museum — was unspeakable."

"The details, Mary Lou, the details," Horace interrupted. "Did you bring my — I mean, your — notes?"

"Why, yes I did. And it was awfully hard taking them, too, the museum being dark and all. But here goes." She opened her purse, pulled out a pair of glasses, and unfolded a stapled stack of papers. Raising her head one more time to smile at the audience before she read, Mary Lou suddenly let out a blood-curdling scream and fainted.

Several people rushed to her aid, and someone in the audience shouted, "Get her some water!"

In an instant, Horace snatched the water pitcher on the desk in front of him. Shouting "Out of my way!" he reached over and poured its contents in Mary Lou's face. She sputtered and sat up suddenly, shaking her head so violently that her CD cap fell off.

"What is it, Mary Lou?" Horace asked gently. "What made you scream?"

"Th-there w-was a-a m-monster in th-the w-window," she stammered, pointing to a large expanse of glass on the left wall. "I-it was horrible! He had the ugliest, twisted face, like somebody who was being boiled alive!"

Bertram practically fell on the floor.

"Now, Mary Lou," Horace said as though he were talking to a child, "don't let your imagination run away with you. All the monsters are in that Fear Factory — unless you count the Potters over there, who run it."

Clark immediately jumped up in protest.

"Don't patronize me, Horace Wright," Mary Lou said. "I know what I saw. And I'm telling you, it looked like it belonged in that place."

Bertram's worst fears about the statue were coming true — it was actually at the courthouse! It had probably been attracted by all the noise. Everyone in the tiny town of Black Bayou, Louisiana was at the meeting. Bertram whispered his suspicions to Poppa, who was enjoying the spectacle and didn't seem at all worried, when suddenly the doors at the back of the courtroom were flung open.

Mary Lou screamed again, but this time she didn't faint. Rising from her seat and pointing, she shouted, "That's him! That's the monster!"

Poppa and Bertram jumped up and ran toward the door. The statue looked their way, as if he recognized them and knew what they were up to, and fled instantly.

— Six —

By the time Bertram and Poppa got out into the corridor, the monster was nowhere to be seen.

"Now, where could he have gone so fast?" Poppa asked.

"How about if we check the bathrooms?" Bertram suggested, pointing to two doors at the end of the hall.

"Good idea. Go ahead."

Bertram grimaced and raced down the hall. He looked in the men's room first — it was empty. After hesitating for a moment, he opened the door to the ladies' room and quickly looked around. Fortunately for him, it was empty, too. He hurried back to Poppa.

"I guess he must have gone out the door," Bertram said, out of breath. By now, a number of people had piled out of the courtroom and seemed about to launch search parties of their own.

"Let's get out of here before your parents see us," Poppa suggested. "Maybe Siggy saw where our statue went."

But outside the courtroom Sigmund was fast asleep, his head leaning on the steering wheel.

"Some getaway," Bertram complained.

"Wake up, Siggy. Siggy, wake up!" Poppa half sang. Sigmund could stay awake for amazingly long periods of time without showing signs of fatigue. But when he finally did fall asleep, he went into a deep sleep, almost like a trance.

With no response from Sigmund, Poppa shouted right in Siggy's ear. The little man awoke with a start, his head jerking back against the seat. He looked at Poppa and Bertram through glazed eyes as if he had never seen them before.

"Siggy, he's here! The statue's here!" Poppa shouted. "If you hadn't fallen asleep, we would have had him!"

Poppa could have been talking backward for all the recognition he got from Siggy. "Siggy, it is I, Phineas Potter, and this is Bertram," he said in a loud voice. "We are wearing costumes, and we are standing out in the courthouse parking lot, waiting for you to wake up so we can look for the statue that ran away from the factory. Now, wake up and start the car!"

But Siggy just stared at the windshield. Poppa reached into the car and gave his face a little slap. Siggy jumped, but he didn't seem much more awake than before.

"It's useless," said Poppa. "Help me push him over, and I'll drive."

"But Poppa, you promised you wouldn't!"

"I know, but this is an emergency," Poppa said.

"Look, since we don't know where the statue went and we can't chase him in any one direction, why don't we go back inside and see what's happening?" Bertram suggested.

"I suppose you're right — again," Poppa said. "How did you get so wise? Not from your father, I'll tell you."

They left Sigmund in the car to doze off again, and trekked back across the parking lot to the courthouse.

Inside, the commotion continued. Horace started banging the gavel again, and finally regained control of the crowd. Bertram and Poppa took their former seats without being noticed.

Horace cleared his throat loudly. "Well, folks, this little display proves that these folks shouldn't be allowed to operate that so-called museum of theirs. If they can disrupt a serious town meeting with a juvenile prank like that — getting somebody to dress up like one of their monstrous statues — then I say they don't belong in our town!"

"Now, wait a minute!" Bertram's father shouted. "I appeal to the good sense of the people of this town. If we wanted to get your support, why would we invite someone dressed as a monster to disrupt the meeting? How would it serve our purpose? The one who has the most to gain from this kind of prank is Horace Q. Wright — and his Citizens for Decency. Why don't you ask *him* if he knows anything about the monster?"

Horace glared at him and rapped his gavel sharply on the desk. "That's enough out of you, Mr. Potter. You can't go around making accusations like that without evidence."

"Shut up, Horace!" someone shouted. "He's right. What would he have to gain by asking a monster to come by?"

"Yeah, Horace," someone else said. "How do we know you didn't invite the monster yourself?"

Horace stared fiercely at the man. "Because, my dear citizens, who else but the Potters could make such a grotesque mask and costume? If I had that kind of talent, I'd open a waxworks myself!" he declared.

Horace's mouth obviously worked faster than his brain. At least he was smart enough not to make it worse by trying to take it back. He could sense he had already lost the crowd.

"Way to go, Horace!" one person cried.

"Go home, Horace!" another called out.

Horace turned beet-red. "This meeting is hereby adjourned," he announced. "But you haven't heard the end of this yet!"

"Let's go," Bertram whispered to Poppa. "We'd better get home before Mom and Dad or we'll be dead meat."

He practically pushed Poppa off the bench and they headed straight for the exit, while the group continued to taunt Horace.

This time, Siggy was awake, and the motor was idling. "Home, quick!" Poppa shouted to him.

"We'd better get as much of our costumes off in the car as we can," Bertram said. "I brought some makeup remover."

"Excellent thinking!" Poppa agreed.

By the time they reached the Fear Factory, they were practically transformed back into their usual selves. "A little soap and water and we'll be as good as new," Poppa predicted.

"It's a good thing," said Bertram. "We don't have a second to lose."

Poppa and Siggy slipped off to their rooms and Bertram ran upstairs to change into his pajamas. He was just coming out of the bathroom when he heard his parents trudge through the front door. He ran downstairs as if he had been waiting all night for them to return.

"How was the meeting?" he asked. "Did anything happen? How many people were there? Are they going to close us down?" Bertram rubbed his eyes sleepily for effect.

"Whoa, ease off, son," his father said. "Just calm down a minute, and we'll tell you everything," he promised. "You should have been there, Bertram."

"You wouldn't let me go," Bertram reminded his father.

"That's right. No, what I meant was, it was super."

"*Super,* Dad? When are you going to stop using words like *super*?"

"What difference does it make? Anyhow, it was great. Horace couldn't keep order, not even after he fired off a gun, and — "

"A gun?" Bertram pretended to be shocked.

His father related the events of the evening, but he made it sound almost boring compared to what had really happened.

"Imagine that. Horace actually thought *we* were behind that monster." Mr. Potter chuckled, poking Bertram's mother in the ribs. "Isn't that a hoot?"

Marie Potter giggled.

But Bertram didn't find the incident amusing at all. He and Poppa *had* created the monster, and if anyone found out, they'd be in big trouble. Poppa might even have to go to jail, or something like that.

There was only one thing to do: find The Man Being Boiled Alive before it found anyone else!

— Seven —

After saying goodnight, Bertram went upstairs to his room. But he couldn't fall asleep. He felt awful. It was his fault that the whole family was in such trouble. However, if it hadn't been for his experiment, they never would have known that Poppa's X-13 formula was a success.

Tired of tossing and turning for the past two hours, Bertram crept downstairs and made his way with a flashlight along the dark halls to Poppa's apartment. To his surprise, when he came around the corner just outside Dora's room, she opened the door. They both jumped.

"Bertram, you scared me. What are you doing down here?" she asked. "Are you hungry? I can fix you a midnight snack, if you like," she offered nicely.

"No, thanks, Dora."

"Well, what's the matter? Can't you sleep?" Dora asked.

Bertram shrugged. "Not really. Dora, I have a big problem," he said quietly. "You'll never believe what happened tonight."

"Oh, I don't know about that." Dora chuckled. "I've seen some awfully strange things around here during the past twenty years. Try me."

Bertram quickly explained the creation of the new statue, The Man Being Boiled Alive, and how he had actually come alive with the X-13. Dora's eyebrows raised a few times during the story, but she didn't seem all that surprised. She and Poppa had been friends for a long time, and she was the only other person besides Bertram who respected Poppa's scientific — and magical — ability.

"Well, you should be pleased with the results — but scared, too." Dora shook her head. "You've gotten yourselves into deep trouble. But look on the bright side. If you and Poppa were clever enough to get into this mess, then the two of you are clever enough to figure a way of getting out of it."

"I guess you're right," Bertram said. "As long as my parents don't find out what's going on."

"I wouldn't worry about that," Dora replied. "They can be pretty blind about things around here — other than the annual report, that is. And you can count on me to distract them, if need be. But if you ever tell them I said that, I'll deny it." She winked and smiled at Bertram. "Remember, if you need me, you can count on old Dora."

"Thanks. I feel a little better. I think I'll go see what Poppa's up to. Good night!" Bertram said, skipping down the hall.

"Don't stay up too late!" Dora whispered loudly. When Bertram reached Poppa's apartment, he could hear a Viennese waltz playing on the tape deck. He rapped loudly on the door.

The door opened only a few seconds later. "I was expecting you," Poppa said warmly. He seemed to be in high spirits. "You know, I still can't believe the X-13 worked. However, I must say that I'm a bit worried about The Man's behavior."

"That's why we have to do something," Bertram said earnestly.

"Now?" Poppa asked.

Bertram nodded.

"Can't it wait until morning?"

"No, it can't. By then it might be too late," Bertram said sadly.

"Well, we could kill some time by having our full-moon ceremony," Poppa suggested half-heartedly.

Bertram clapped his hands together. "That's it!" he shouted. "In addition to my mixing the X-13 right into the wax, it took the full moon to get it going. Do you think that when the moon starts to wane that The Man Being Boiled Alive will stop walking, or come home?"

"How am I supposed to know?" Poppa said. "I only mixed the formula, I didn't invent it."

"Well, if you're not sure then we really can't wait. Let's get Siggy and go look for the statue."

"You know, you're doing all right for yourself in the thinking department," Poppa observed. "Let's get our chauffeur!"

Bertram and Poppa headed right for Siggy's room, but it took several minutes of steady pounding on the door until they roused him. He appeared at the door with his hair more rumpled than usual, but wearing a maroon silk robe over a pair of blue-and-white-striped pajamas.

"Now vat?" Siggy said in a sleepy voice, stretching his arms over his head. "This better be more important than sleep."

"If you value your job, you will get dressed at once and take us out to find that walking statue," Poppa said.

"I vas afraid of someting like zat. Vait here."

In less than five minutes, Siggy dressed and they sneaked out of the museum to the back where the convertible was parked. "What a night for hunting!" Poppa exclaimed. "A full moon and everything."

"Better vatch out for verevolves and vampires," Siggy said. He laughed an evil laugh.

Siggy maneuvered the car carefully through the deserted streets of Black Bayou. They did not pass another vehicle for ten minutes, and then it was only a long-distance tractor trailer heading for the Interstate. Now and then the car's headlights reflected off of an animal's eyes as it scurried along the side of the road — raccoons, a possum or two and a badger.

Poppa turned around. "If you were a walking waxwork, where would you go?" he asked Bertram.

Bertram searched his memory of old horror movies and comics, and couldn't remember ever seeing anything like it before. "I know where I wouldn't go — to a sauna," he said.

"Yes, that's true. It is a puzzle to me what this statue uses to think with," Poppa said. "We can assume it doesn't think, at least not the way we know. It must be receiving some kind of electric stimulation caused by the interaction of the X-13 with the wax."

"A what?" Bertram asked.

"A kind of energy that changed inanimate objects into the first life on earth," Poppa explained. "It doesn't involve thinking. Lots of lower life forms on earth still rely on that kind of reaction."

"Like Horace Q. Wright?" Bertram joked.

"Well, it's good to see you haven't lost your sense of humor. That may be the only thing we have left after this mess is over," Poppa said glumly.

Siggy, who had not said anything for minutes, suddenly let loose with a torrent of German words.

"What is it, Siggy?" Poppa asked. "What's wrong?"

"I just go through a red light, and vouldn't you know it, a cop car is following us."

"Well, you'd better pull over," Poppa said.

Bertram shrank down in the back seat. He had a feeling that this was going to be one of the worst nights of his life.

Siggy pulled the convertible over to the curb, and the police car stopped behind it.

"Good evening, officer," Poppa said cheerfully. "What seems to be the problem?"

"Moving violation. You ran a red light back there. Didn't you see that it was red?" he asked Siggy.

Siggy shook his head.

"I need to see your driver's license, please," the officer said politely.

Siggy reached into his back pocket and after much fumbling produced an old crumbly-looking wallet. He handed his license to the officer and grinned.

But the officer didn't look nearly as happy. "I can't read this. It's some foreign driver's license," he complained. "From what I can make out, it looks like it expired twenty-five years ago."

Siggy looked incredulously at the driver's license. "Yes, this is from Germany. But officer, I do haf a Louisiana license," he protested. "I just don't know vere it is."

"I'm afraid I'll have to bring you down to the station house," the officer said. "This is a pretty serious charge — driving without a valid license. After I pull out ahead of you, please follow me," he instructed Siggy.

They followed the police car in silence to the station house, about a mile away. There were only a handful of officers on duty, and at least one of them seemed to be asleep. In addition, there was a young woman who sat leaning against a dull-green wall. She looked extremely bored.

Bertram, Poppa, and Siggy stopped at the front desk, where a large sergeant was stapling piles of paper together. "What can I do for you?" he said without looking up.

"They're with me, Smitty, " the patrol officer explained.

Smitty finally looked up. "Hey, Ralph. What are they in for? Kidnapping the boy?"

"Not that I know of, although I really don't know what he's doing out at this time of the night," Ralph said.

"Didn't you ask him?" Smitty said.

"No."

"Would you care to explain?" Smitty asked Bertram.

Bertram glanced at Poppa, then back at the policemen. "Uh, this is my grandfather," he said nervously. "We're on a rescue mission."

"No kidding!" Smitty exclaimed. "And just what are you rescuing?"

"Well, it's kind of a long story," Bertram said.

"I got all night," Smitty told him, leaning back in his chair. "Go on."

Bertram looked at Poppa again. Poppa nodded at him. "It's okay, Bertram. Tell him everything," he said solemnly. "Maybe they'll be able to help us."

So for the second time that night Bertram explained about The Man Being Boiled Alive and the X-13 and how a monster was now roaming around Black Bayou and how it was his responsibility to catch him.

The officers were surprised by the story — but not in the way Bertram thought they would be. Instead of acting concerned for the safety of their town, they seemed to find it all very amusing. Bertram couldn't even get in the part about the monster showing up at the courthouse because they were laughing so hard.

Ralph and Smitty's whoops of laughter brought the bored young woman and one of the dozing officers over to the desk.

"What's so funny, Smitty?" the young woman asked.

"Listen to this," Sergeant Smith said between guffaws. He proceeded to tell her Bertram and Poppa's story.

She giggled a little, but in general she seemed intrigued by the news. "Well," she said, "I'm not sure whether this is true or not, but I can report that somebody *thinks* it's true. And that's good enough for the morning edition of *The Leader*.

The Leader! Bertram thought to himself. That was the newspaper published by Horace Q. Wright. If he got ahold of their story, he'd have all the ammunition he needed to finish off the Fear Factory — for good!

— Eight —

"What are you doing, April? Writing a story for the newspaper?" Sergeant Smith leaned over his desk at the notebook the reporter was holding.

"Yes. Do you have any objections?" she asked.

"Only that these two guys are harmless crackpots. I think the kid has just gotten carried away by their raving, and now he believes this stuff, too. Can you imagine a statue getting up and walking across town?"

"Frankly, no," April replied. "But I do happen to know that Mr. Wright is trying to shut these guys down, and if I can help in some way, maybe I'll get promoted off the precinct night beat."

"And I thought you loved us," Smitty said, pouting.

"I'd love you even more if I could stop by and visit — during regular work hours like a normal person," April said, yawning. Her eyes looked glassy.

70

"Listen, how about if you knock off now and if anything happens, I'll give you a call," the sergeant offered.

April hesitated.

"If I were you, I wouldn't send my boss a lunatic story like this," Ralph commented. "You might want to pretend that you didn't hear anything about it. He'll think you fell asleep on the job and dreamed the whole thing!"

"You're probably right," April agreed. "After all, it is the full moon. Call me if you see a werewolf, okay?" She gave the sergeant her phone number and left the precinct house.

Sergeant Smith looked at Poppa and Siggy. "I hate to do this, folks. If the boy weren't involved, I'd just let you two crazies go. But I feel it's my duty to call the boy's parents."

Bertram felt his palms start to sweat. "But Poppa here is my grandfather," he reminded the sergeant. "He can make sure I get home safe and sound."

Poppa nodded vigorously. "Yes, we'll just walk. It's a nice night. Someone can come down tomorrow and pick up the car."

"I don't think so, buddy," Sergeant Smith said. "For one thing, it's two o'clock in the morning — a little late to be walking around Black Bayou. And for another, how do I know you're the boy's grandfather? You don't have any I.D. on you, and if you were his grandfather, why would you take him out in a convertible in the middle of the night?"

"We've already explained. that," Bertram said.

"Yeah, yeah, I know — you had to chase the walking statue. What's your phone number, kid?"

Bertram sighed. "It's 555-FEAR."

As the sergeant dialed the phone, Poppa leaned over and whispered to Bertram, "I hope your father wakes up in a good mood."

"Mr. Potter? This is Sergeant Smith down at the First Precinct. Yes, nothing to worry about. Your son is down here and we thought you might like to pick him up. No, no, he's all right. There's a man here claiming to be his grandfather. You'll be right down? Good."

Fifteen minutes later, Bertram's parents walked through the front door of the station house. They had both thrown long coats on over their pajamas and they looked rumpled — and upset.

Bertram tried to look sorry, but he could hardly hide his amusement. Maybe it was because he was finally getting sleepy, but everything that had seemed so serious a half hour earlier, now seemed only ridiculous, even funny. He knew his parents were going to yell at him, but he didn't care.

Fortunately all his mother said was, "We'll talk about this in the morning."

"I'll drive the convertible home. The rest of you go with Marie in our car," his father said in a monotone.

When Bertram got home, he fell immediately into bed and slept soundly until the alarm went off. As he was lying there, he began to remember the incidents of the previous night. He sat up abruptly and jumped out of bed. There was so much to do! He dressed quickly and ran downstairs to the kitchen, where Dora had a plate of pancakes waiting for him.

As Bertram wolfed down his breakfast, his father came into the room and sat down across the table from him. *Uh oh,* Bertram thought to himself, *here it comes.*

"Now, Bertram," Mr. Potter said solemnly. "I'm not going to ask what you were doing riding around with Siggy and Poppa last night. I know you'd only make up some ridiculous excuse, and frankly, I don't want to know what you three were up to. But it was dangerous for you to be out so late. Now, your mother and I don't want to forbid you from seeing Poppa, but we think that, sooner or later, we may have no other choice. You can't continue to get wrapped up in his escapades — one so-called magician in the family is enough. Do you understand me?"

Bertram picked at his breakfast. "Yes," he answered. "But I still think Poppa has a lot to teach me."

"About wax figures, yes," his father agreed. "About taking joy rides in the middle of the night, no. Now, I hate to do this, but I'm afraid I'm going to have to ground you, for the next few days at least. I want you to come home right after school and I want you to stay in your room — that means no going to Poppa's lab, either. Am I making myself clear?"

Bertram nodded. He had heard the same lecture many times before — he practically had it memorized. Every time his parents grounded him, he found a way to get around it — and today was no exception. Once his father had gone back into his office, Bertram pretended to leave for school — but he quickly turned around and re-entered the Fear Factory through a side door that he kept unlocked for emergencies just like this.

"Cheer up," Poppa said when Bertram told him about being grounded. "What they don't know won't hurt them. At least that April woman didn't write the story for *The Leader*."

"I know. But we're not even close to finding The Man Being Boiled Alive," Bertram said, "and now it'll be even harder for me to help you look for him. What if he shows up somewhere today?"

"I'll listen to the police band. If anything will have news about him, that will," Poppa said.

"In that case, if he turns up, do you promise you'll come and get me out of school?"

"How can I do that?"

"Oh, I don't know. Tell them that my little baby brother can't be found, and that I have to come home right away," Bertram suggested.

"But you don't have a brother," Poppa said.

"That's just the point. I'll understand the code, and I won't have to feel bad that you lied to the principal, because I don't have a brother," Bertram said triumphantly.

Poppa stared at Bertram as if he didn't understand.

"What if the police capture the statue?" Bertram asked. "Then they'll know we were telling the truth. But Horace Q. Wright will also have enough evidence to close our doors."

"Don't worry about it," Poppa said. "What man would turn himself over to the police? Even a statue wouldn't be so stupid."

"You're right — we've got to give our creation some credit, I guess. Well, let me know what happens. I have to take off for school now," Bertram said.

"Have a good day," Poppa said. "And don't worry. Everything's under control."

But Bertram knew there was nothing farther from the truth!

Nothing happened all day. In fact, nothing happened all weekend. Business at the Fear Factory went on as usual. In an account of the town meeting, the local newspaper offered the theory that "the monster was apparently someone's horrifying idea of a joke." But other than that, no mention was made of the creature's appearance. It was as if everyone in the whole town had forgotten Thursday night's episode. Everyone, that is, except Bertram, his grandfather and his grandfather's assistant.

"Maybe he drown in bayou," suggested Siggy Sunday night after dinner. Bertram was no longer grounded, and he was hanging out in the lab with Siggy and Poppa.

"Or maybe he went to another town," Bertram added.

"If he showed up in another town, we would have heard about it by now," Poppa said. "News travels very fast. The statue is probably hiding out somewhere."

"That means it can think!" Bertram cried excitely.

"Probably better than half the people in this town." Poppa chuckled. "No, actually I have no information that leads me to believe it can do anything besides walk and look fierce. That much we know ourselves."

"I just hope it doesn't walk into the wrong person," Bertram said.

On Monday after school, Wesley and Bertram did their social studies homework together at Bertram's house. They polished off their work quickly, then read some new comics that Wesley had brought over. Bertram, who was a faster reader, finished first and then began playing with a ball of soft wax, fashioning it into a miniature figure, while Wesley continued to read.

As Bertram worked the wax, he reached over and tuned into the police radio channel. Nothing much was going on. He was just about to turn it off when a bulletin came in:

"Car Four to Station. Car Four to Station. We just responded to a complaint at 1240 Kingfisher. Maybelle Leclerc has reported that she saw the guy in the monster outfit from the meeting the other night. She said she was in her kitchen when he came onto her back porch, where she was cooling some apple pies. He stole one right off the table. She chased him with a broom, but he got away with the pie."

"Fantastic!" Bertram shouted. "That means he eats!"

"Of course he eats," Wesley said. "He'll have to take his mask off first, though."

"That isn't any mask," Bertram said. "That 'guy in the monster outfit' is a statue that my grandfather made. When I poured the X-13 into the wax mixture, it gave him the power to walk, but not until it was the full moon."

"Do you actually expect me to believe that?" Wesley scoffed. "I'm not five years old, you know. You might get away with that stuff with my two sisters, but even they would probably laugh in your face."

"All right, if you don't believe me, then I'll take you down to where we were keeping the statue. You'll see that it isn't there anymore."

"So what does that prove?" Wesley challenged. "I never saw the statue in the first place. For all I know, it never even existed. Or maybe somebody moved it."

"Are you calling me a liar, Wesley Fairchild?"

Before Wesley could answer, there was a frantic knocking at Bertram's door and Poppa ran in, a look of crazed excitement on his face.

"You heard it, too?" Bertram asked.

Poppa, unable to talk, nodded wildly. He gestured for the boys to follow him. Scooping up their jackets, they made their way through the corridors of the Fear Factory to Sigmund's apartment, where the assistant was waiting.

Before they knew it, the boys were sitting in the back of the old convertible, with Poppa in the front next to Siggy at the wheel. Maybelle Leclerc lived on the opposite side of town. Poppa held an open map on his lap and started barking directions at Siggy.

"Right out of the driveway, to Bowie. Up Bowie to Loyola, left on Loyola to Delta Boulevard, two miles to Kingfisher, then a right."

As they drove up Kingfisher, just before they came to the old wooden bridge, they passed a police car parked by the curb. Bertram thought there was something familiar about the officer's face he saw through the window. "Poppa," he said, "the police officer who caught us for skipping the red light was in that parked police car! What if he sees us?"

"It's all right," Poppa said. "Sigmund found his Louisiana driver's license. He actually had it the whole time. It was in his wallet behind his Bela Lugosi autograph. How it got there, he doesn't know."

"But remember what he said?" Bertram protested. "He thinks you're a crackpot. He'll think we're here chasing the statue."

"Well, we are, aren't we?" Poppa asked.

"Yes, but — I don't know, I just have a bad feeling about this. I think they're going to keep an eye on us, no matter what we do. They'll probably follow us. And if they tell Mom and Dad . . . "

"Okay, Bertram. Maybe you're right. We'll just get out of his sight as quickly as possible," Poppa said.

Siggy misinterpreted Poppa's words. He stopped the car in the middle of the block, made a U-turn and began to speed off in the opposite direction.

"Where are you going?" Poppa demanded.

"You say get out of sight, I get out of sight," Siggy replied.

"No, that's not what I meant," Poppa said.

"Make up your mind," Siggy said as they passed the police car again on their way back down the street. "Should I turn around here?"

"Oh, just forget it!" Poppa said. "We're not going to pass him a third time. That's an invitation to disaster."

Siggy retraced their route across town, only faster, and they soon pulled into the driveway of the Fear Factory. When Bertram got out of the car, he realized that he had been holding his breath almost the whole way home, he was so nervous.

"Some adventure," Wesley said bitterly. "I still say that statue doesn't even exist — much less walk."

"Just because we didn't see him doesn't mean he doesn't exist," Bertram argued.

"Oh, and I suppose next you'll be telling me that he's invisible," Wesley said.

As they trudged through the front door, their argument was cut short by Dora, who was waiting for them. "You're not going to believe what's been going on in the last hour," she told Bertram. "If you think things were bad before, wait till you hear the trouble you're in now!"

— Nine —

"What is it?" Bertram asked. He felt his heart starting to beat faster.

"Horace Q. Wright came on the radio this afternoon, on the *Around Black Bayou* show, to talk about closing us down, and the meeting Thursday. He said he had just gotten a news report about a monster stealing an apple pie across town. You wouldn't know anything about that, now, would you?"

Before Bertram had a chance to answer, Dora continued. "Anyway, he came right out and blamed your parents for this 'latest assault,' as he calls it. And that's not all. It seems that a reporter for *The Leader* told him some incredible story about an old man who's taking credit for the monster. She said the police thought he was a harmless crackpot, but Horace thinks otherwise himself. He can't wait to get proof and press charges. After that, your mom and dad got on the phone to their lawyer, and that's where they are right now. They think they have a good lawsuit against Horace for defamation of character."

"Did you try to stop them?" Poppa asked. "Did you tell them the truth?"

"What, and admit I believe you built a wax statue that is now walking around town, stealing apple pies? They'd think I was crazy. No, I like my job. I like my freedom. I'm not ready to spend the rest of my days in the Shady Hollow Sanitarium."

"I see your point," Poppa said thoughtfully.

"Then this calls for action!" Bertram shouted. "We have to be the ones who bring in The Man Being Boiled Alive. Otherwise, I could go to jail for the rest of my life."

"Don't panic," Poppa said. "We'll just go out like a real search party. Now that we know that The Man is still in town, it shouldn't be so hard."

"Maybe not if we had an army," Bertram said. He was afraid that the situation was hopeless.

"Well, at least we can go out in two cars," Dora said. "I'll drive my car — that should help the search go faster. I want you to find that statue and bring him back here. I don't want to have to send cookies to you when you're behind bars. You know, I bet if you ask your friend Adelaide, she'll help out."

Wesley made a sour face at the mention of the girl's name. Bertram wrinkled his nose.

"Don't be too picky," Dora said. "You need all the help you can get. At least Adelaide can be counted on not to squeal to the police. And she'll believe anything, the wilder the better."

Adelaide was in the same class as Bertram and Wesley, and she had caused a stir in school when she appeared on the first day. First of all, her first and last names were exactly alike, which caused a great deal of laughter during roll call. Also, she had a wide magenta streak down the center of her long blond hair. She had just moved to Black Bayou from Brooklyn, New York, and she was very different from the rest of the kids in town.

"I just can't stand that whiny voice of hers," Wesley said. "If she goes, I don't."

"Well, you can be in separate cars," Dora suggested.

"I'm going with Wesley," Bertram said. "How about if the boys go out in one car and the girls in the other?"

"No, because you'll have four people and we'll have only two," Dora argued. "And if this so-called monster is really a monster, we won't be strong enough to hold on to him. One of you has to come with me. I think it would be a good idea for Poppa and Siggy to stay together."

"Oh, all right," Bertram agreed. "I'll come with you." He was just as glad not to have to

84

ride with Siggy, whose driving he didn't trust. Dora was a good, sensible driver.

A few minutes later, they pulled up in front of Adelaide's house. It was just after five o'clock, and she was returning from her paper route. "Hey, what's up?" she asked. "Are you guys leaving town or something?" She looked at the two cars, obviously confused — especially by Siggy's appearance behind the wheel of the convertible. "Or is this an early Halloween parade?" she asked.

"Very funny," Wesley replied. "You should be a comedienne when you grow up."

Bertram glared at Wesley as he got out of the car. "Actually, Adelaide, we need to ask you a favor," he said as nicely as he could. "Do you have a few minutes?"

"That depends," she said. "Will it be fun?"

Bertram laughed. "Well, uh, maybe," he said. Then he gave her the shortest possible version of what had happened with the X-13, and why they were in two separate cars.

"I love car chases!" Adelaide exclaimed. "We had them all the time in Brooklyn." She turned toward her house and shouted, "Be right back, Mom!" Then she jumped into Dora's car, right behind Bertram and said, "Let's go!"

"I've never seen a person being boiled alive," she went on as they started driving down the street. "Although I once saw someone fall into a vat of hot tar while the Department of Streets was making repairs in Brooklyn. And then there was the time the man fell into the open storm sewer. He just slipped because the street was wet and the next thing he knew . . . "

Bertram stopped listening. Adelaide knew about ten times more horrible things that had happened to people than any other kid. He was sure that she made up half of the stuff. Since no one else in Black Bayou came from Brooklyn, they couldn't tell if she was lying or not about the strange things that supposedly went on there.

Dora headed across town, back to the area near Maybelle Leclerc's house, while Siggy and Poppa drove up and down the east side, where the Fear Factory was located.

There was no sign of The Man outside or around the Leclerc house, so Dora slowly cruised the streets nearby. They went all the way to the town limits, then circled back and crossed the old wooden bridge over the creek. As they came to an intersection and stopped for a red light, Adelaide suddenly said, "Hey, look at that!"

"Look at what?" Bertram asked.

"It looks like something is going on inside that diner." She pointed toward Bud and Lou's

Diner, one of Black Bayou's finest dining establishments.

Against the fading daylight, the interior was barely visible from the street. But Adelaide prided herself on her keen eyesight. "Something's going on over there, I can tell!" she announced.

Dora drove through the intersection and pulled into the parking lot outside the diner. They quickly got out of the car and ran over to the glass entrance door. As they peered through it, they saw an amazing sight. The Man Being Boiled Alive was standing behind the counter next to a huge refrigerator, wolfing down its contents. The people in the diner were cowering behind tables and booths.

First The Man practically inhaled a whole lemon meringue pie. Then he moved on to a large container of rice pudding, which he seemed to swallow in one big gulp. He followed that up with a whole honeydew melon, rind and all.

"His appetite reminds me a little of yours," Dora said jokingly to Bertram.

"You know," Adelaide said, "we never decided what we would do with this creature when we found him. But I don't know if we can catch him, especially now that he's eaten all that food."

"You're right," Bertram said. "But I guess we could try throwing boiling water on him — lots of it. That will finish him off, for sure. They should have lots of boiling water in the kitchen. I'm going to take a shot at it." Dora and Adelaide tried to hold Bertram back, but he was so proud of his idea and eager to catch the creature that he wriggled out of their grasp and boldly strode into the diner.

The moment Bertram walked in, The Man Being Boiled Alive looked up from the vat of chili he was about to devour. He started, as if he recognized Bertram, then threw down the pot of chili and backed away toward the front of the diner. As Bertram moved closer, the people in the diner whispered, "Be careful!" "Don't do it!" and "He's an animal!"

But Bertram wasn't afraid. He took another step toward the monster when suddenly, The Man turned and leaped straight through the plate-glass window at the front of the diner. Several people screamed.

"Bertram, he's getting away!" Adelaide shouted from outside.

Racing out the door, Bertram saw The Man disappear into some trees at the far end of a field behind the diner. "Let's go after him!" he yelled.

He, Adelaide and Dora piled into Dora's car and sped off in the direction they saw The Man go. They were heading toward the town park.

"If we lose him in there, we won't be able to do a thing until tomorrow," Bertram said, disappointed he hadn't grabbed the statue when he had the chance. "It's going to be dark soon."

Suddenly, a car pulled out right in front of them. Dora slammed on the brakes and the car screeched to a stop just inches from — Poppa and Siggy in the convertible. Bertram groaned. So far, the big search party was a disaster!

Dora pulled off to the side of the road, and Siggy turned around and came up beside them.

"Land sakes alive!" Dora shouted out the window. "What are you trying to do?"

Poppa got out of the car and came over to her window. "Where are you off to in such a hurry?" he asked, as if they were just out for a Sunday drive.

"We saw him at the diner!" Bertram shouted. "And now you've made us lose him!"

"You mean our Man was at Bud and Lou's?" Poppa asked, becoming visibly excited.

"Yes, eating everything in sight. Now he's gone, thanks to Siggy," Bertram said.

Siggy hung his head in shame. "Don't be so hard on him," Dora said. "After all, we thought we were on the trail. We haven't seen

90

The Man since he disappeared into those trees back near the diner."

"Dora's right," Adelaide agreed. Bertram wished they hadn't brought her along — although she had been the one to spot the statue. He had to give her some credit.

"Okay, I'm sorry," Bertram said, realizing an apology was called for. "It's not your fault, Siggy." Siggy's mouth curved into a crooked smile.

Before they could decide what to do next, the sound of police sirens suddenly filled the air.

"I hope nobody's been following us!" Dora exclaimed. "The last thing I need is a speeding ticket."

"No, I think the sirens are coming from the other way," Bertram said. Sure enough, two police cars came speeding down the opposite side of the street in the direction of the diner. "I guess somebody at the diner finally decided it was safe enough to come out from under the tables and call the police."

"Maybe," Wesley said, "but I just heard over the radio that there was a bank robbery downtown. They're probably headed to Main Street."

"Hmm . . . " Bertram mused. "If the police are tied up with a robbery, then they can't pay much attention to a man they think is dressed as a monster, can they? That'll give us a chance to find him first."

"Excellent!" Adelaide said. "Now this is getting exciting."

"You know," Poppa said, "I wonder if we ought to stick together this time. There's strength in numbers, after all."

Bertram guessed that Poppa had had enough of Siggy's driving, too.

"How about if we all squeeze into Dora's car? We can park the convertible here and pick it up on the way home," Poppa suggested.

"Vat do you vant to do that for?" Siggy asked. "I haf fun driving around like detective on television."

"Yes, but you almost killed us," Dora reminded him.

"Oh, all right," Siggy said. "But I vant to sit in front."

It was just about dark now, and as they squeezed into Dora's old station wagon, Bertram realized that they didn't have much time left. They drove east, each person peering out the window for any signs of The Man Being Boiled Alive. They crossed Loyola and pulled up to a red light at the corner of Bailey.

As Bertram looked over at a car wash across the street, his pulse began to race. "There he is!" he shouted, pointing to a blue sedan that was just ready to be ushered into the building.

The statue had opened the front door on the passenger's side and was climbing in. A terrified middle-aged man jumped out of the driver's side and took off running at top speed, abandoning his car. An attendant looked on with confusion, his eyes wide with surprise.

"We should have known!" Bertram said. "Where else would a person who was being boiled want to go?"

"Hurry, Dora!" Poppa yelled. "We can catch him when he comes out!"

— Ten —

Bertram, Poppa, Sigmund, Dora, Adelaide, and Wesley all jumped out of the car and raced around to the car wash exit. "Somebody should cover the entrance, too!" Bertram shouted, as he and Wesley started to head toward the spot where The Man had gotten into the sedan. But when they turned the corner, they saw The Man Being Boiled Alive dashing across the parking lot to the shopping mall next door.

"Don't lose him!" Wesley shouted. "I'll call the others!"

Bertram followed The Man into the shopping mall and saw him disappear into the Sixplex movie theaters. He ran back out and waited outside the mall entrance until Wesley and the others caught up with him.

"Movie theater!" he said breathlessly, pointing the way. The group entered the mall and headed straight for the theater lobby.

"What's weird is that nobody else seems to have seen him come in," Bertram said. "Nobody is acting like anything strange happened.

94

I mean, it isn't every day that a hideous statue visits a shopping mall."

"Maybe they were more scared by Adelaide," Wesley suggested, an evil grin on his face.

"Ha ha," Adelaide said. "At least I know not to wear a plaid shirt and striped pants!"

Bertram stifled a laugh. Wesley was just about the worst dresser he had ever seen, but he wanted him on his side for now. Besides, Wesley was his best friend. He didn't care what he wore. He had the best collection of comics of anybody in the sixth grade.

Wesley looked down at his clothes and shrugged. "At least I don't have striped hair," he retorted.

"Okay, kids, cut it out," Dora said. "We have a mission to complete."

"I'll ask the box office cashier if she saw anything," Bertram said. He stepped up to the desk. "Excuse me, but did you see a horrible-looking creature about six and a half feet tall come through here a few minutes ago?"

"Honey," she said with no surprise in her voice, "I've seen a lot of horrible-looking creatures come through these doors, but none in the last few minutes that was six and a half feet tall."

"Thanks." Bertram motioned for everyone to move closer for a conference. "All right, now what do we do?" he asked.

"How about if we split up and each of us takes a theater?" Adelaide suggested. "We can all agree to meet out here in, say, fifteen minutes."

"Sounds good to me," Poppa said.

They all lined up and each person bought a ticket for a different movie. The Six-plex was deserted because it was so early in the evening, and some of the movies hadn't even started yet. Bertram was lucky; he got a theater where a new horror movie was playing. It seemed like it was almost over.

As Bertram wandered up and down the aisles, searching for The Man Being Boiled Alive, he glanced up at the screen a few times. It made his job a bit more pleasant, but Bertram couldn't watch long enough to actually figure out what was going on. He was in a horror movie of his own!

Bertram had fully expected to find The Man in his theater, and was disappointed when he returned to the lobby with only a wad of chewing gum stuck to the sole of his sneaker.

"Maybe he escaped through one of the back doors," Adelaide said as she emerged from theater number three, which was just now officially opening its doors.

"You mean we might have spent our money on these tickets for nothing?" Bertram asked.

"We don't have enough people to cover all the exits, like in those police shows," Adelaide pointed out.

Bertram was feeling hopeless by the time everyone else returned to the lobby. No one had met with success. No one had found a single clue or even a single person who had seen The Man.

"Well, we do know one thing. Our Man seems to like food," Dora said. "Why don't we stick around the refreshment stand and see if he shows up?" Everyone seemed to think that was as good an idea as any.

"You know, I'm getting pretty hungry myself," Poppa said. "Maybe I'll have some popcorn."

Bertram nodded. "I want a candy bar."

"Me, too!" Wesley said loudly.

"Now, now, don't spoil your appetites," Dora warned. "It won't be long before dinner — " Dora stopped speaking and her eyes filled with fear. "Oh, no! Dinner!" she cried. "I got so wound up with all this that I clean forgot about your folks." She glanced at her watch. "It's 6:15 and I always have dinner for them at 6:00. They hate it when I'm late — you know how funny they are about stuff like that," she said to Bertram. "They're going to be wondering where we *all* are!"

"Uh-oh," he said. "Unless we can come up with an excuse pretty fast, we're all going to be done for."

"How about if I call and tell them — oh, I don't know what we should say." Dora frowned.

"I know," Adelaide said eagerly. "Tell them you had to come out to pick me up — which is exactly what you did. Of course, they'll think you had to pick me up to bring me home, instead of having to pick me up and take me out with you. But you won't really be lying." She knew that Bertram didn't like to lie, whereas she didn't think anything of it — when the situation warranted it.

"Uh, okay," Bertram said. "Here's a quarter. Why don't you call?"

Adelaide went to one of the phones in the middle of the mall opposite the movie lobby and called Bertram's parents. She had his phone number memorized — everyone in Black Bayou did, because it was so easy. Bertram could see her talking in her usual mile-a-minute style. When she hung up, she grinned and flashed them the thumbs-up sign.

As she made her way back to the theater lobby, however, the grin quickly vanished. She started staring at the ticket counter, and Bertram followed her gaze.

Horace Q. Wright and his wife, Nanette, were standing in line. As luck would have it, he spotted them immediately, too.

Horace came storming over to them, waving a finger under Poppa's nose. "You misfits," he said. "You weirdos, you menaces to society. I'll get you, you'll see." Then he and Nanette stormed off into the theater showing the latest horror movie.

"Look at that," Adelaide said as she rejoined the group. "They went into that horror movie."

Poppa let out an indignant huff. "No doubt to see how awful it is so they can warn all decent citizens to stay away from it," he said bitterly.

"Well, that about does it for me," said Dora. "First we lose The Man and then we get yelled at by a complete idiot. What do you say we call it a night?"

But before anyone had a chance to answer, a stampede of people came out of the theater into which Horace and his wife had stepped moments before.

"Two guesses what this is all about!" Adelaide shouted above the din. Bucking the tide, Bertram and Wesley managed to get into the theater, which was just about empty. The movie was still showing as though everything were normal, but otherwise, the room was strangely silent and empty. Bertram looked around for a light switch and found four. He flipped them all on, until the picture was barely visible on the screen and the theater was bright enough to find the runaway statue.

But there was no statue to be found.

"Being a detective is harder than I thought," Wesley admitted. He and Bertram went back out into the lobby, where the rest of the statue-chasing group were being restrained by members of the theater staff.

Horace had obviously convinced the staff that Poppa and his friends were at fault. He stomped his foot on the floor like an angry bull. "I don't care if that's a man dressed up as a monster, or if it's a statue that you made walk," he said to Poppa. "Either way, you're responsible for it. If you'll just admit it, I'll see that the court will go easy on the sentence. You'll probably get off for reason of insanity anyway!"

"I'm not saying anything without my lawyer present," Poppa said in his most dignified voice. "You have absolutely no case against me. Some friends of mine and I decided to take in a movie, that's all." He caught Bertram's eye and winked. "The last time I checked, that wasn't against the law."

A few of the snack bar employees giggled.

"I hope not," the ticket cashier said, "'cause if it is, I'm out of a job!" She let go of Adelaide and returned to the counter.

Horace's face turned bright red. He seemed to realize that he was making a fool of himself. Grabbing his wife's hand, he stormed off, yelling behind him, "I'm going to get you, Phineas Potter!"

"He should be careful," Dora said with a smile. "We could use that threat against him in a court of law."

"Maybe we should just go home and call it a night," Wesley suggested once they had all been let go.

"What if The Man gets into somebody's house and kills him?" Bertram asked.

"Well, it's possible," said Poppa. "But what has he really done so far except scare people with his ugly face, eat large quantities of food and go to the movies?"

"I think if he broke into anyone's house, it would only be to take a shower," Wesley observed. "Or maybe he'd jump in his pool."

Adelaide, who had done a book report on Sigmund Freud and had claimed to be an expert on psychology ever since, said, "I think that The Man probably wants to get close to people. Since everybody is afraid of him, he's lonely. He's just a poor misunderstood monster."

"Who's going to get me thrown in jail for life," Bertram said with a sigh.

They all agreed it was time to head home, and Dora dropped off Poppa and Siggy at the spot where they had left the convertible. "We'll drop Wesley off at home," Dora promised. "Then we'll meet you back at the factory."

Before they got to Wesley's house, they heard the latest radio bulletin by Horace's newsroom, which described the monster's recent appearance at the Six-plex and accused the Potters of being behind it. But the biggest news item of all was a report of a late-season hurricane in the Gulf of Mexico.

"I heard about it this afternoon and I meant to tell you about it," Dora said. "But with all this running around, I forgot. If the hurricane keeps on course, it's expected to hit Black Bayou in two days."

"That's awful," Bertram said. "That means we won't be able to go out and search!"

"I don't think you should worry about that," Dora said, frowning at Bertram. "You should be more concerned about what might happen to the town — to our house."

"Look on the bright side," Wesley said. "Maybe the hurricane will blow The Man Being Boiled Alive right out of town."

"Yes," Dora agreed. "And maybe he'll take Horace Q. Wright with him!"

—— Eleven ——

When Dora pulled up in front of the Fear Factory, Bertram could see his parents staring out the windows of their office on the second floor, overlooking the driveway. "Now we're really going to get it," he said to Dora.

He looked around for the black convertible, but he didn't see it. Siggy and Poppa were still out. They had a knack for disappearing whenever they were in trouble.

He hoped that somehow he could slip into his room without being seen and pretend to fall asleep. But his parents were waiting at the top of the stairs when he and Dora walked in.

"We heard the news report, Bertram," his father said. "And your mother and I are not amused. Adelaide told us you were at the mall, but she didn't mention that you had run into a monster — and Horace Q. Wright — while you were there. What *is* this all about?" he demanded.

"You mean we saw Horace the monster," Dora joked.

"This is no time for jokes!" Mrs. Potter exclaimed. "Explain yourself, Bertram."

"You won't believe me if I tell you that Poppa made a secret formula that brought his new figure to life, even though it's the truth. So what difference does it make what I tell you?" Bertram asked.

"Young man," Bertram's father said sternly, "the last thing we need right now is one of your outrageous stories about Poppa. As punishment for your irresponsible behavior, I forbid you to have anything to do with your grandfather until further notice. I suppose you must see him at mealtime, but you are not to talk to him away from the table. And as for you," he said, turning toward Dora, "I thought you had more sense than to get involved with my father and his harebrained schemes. I don't appreciate your encouraging Bertram to misbehave."

With that, Clark and Marie Potter stalked off.

"I guess they're kind of upset," Bertram said, shrugging.

Dora sighed loudly. "They never want to have any fun. Well, I'd better go fix something to eat. Feel like having some cornbread?"

"Yum!" Bertram cried. "Let's go before they send me to my room without dinner!"

The next day at school everybody was talking about how the monster had shown up to view the latest horror movie in town. Lots of people were talking about the approaching hurricane, too. Kids were so flipped out about what was going on in Black Bayou that they were talking to kids they usually didn't talk to. Some of the students were even talking to the teachers — even to Mr. Rodgers, the principal. Bertram didn't understand the need for such hysteria. A hurricane was only a big rain storm, after all.

During lunch, Bertram felt someone tap him on the back. "Hey Potter, want to buy a T-shirt?"

Bertram looked around and saw Plug Willard, the sixth-grade bully, standing behind him. Plug was holding a stack of T-shirts.

"What do you say, Potter? They're only ten dollars." Plug held one of the T-shirts in front of Bertram's face. There, staring back at him, was The Man Being Boiled Alive.

Bertram felt like saying, "You've got some nerve to try to make money off of *our* statue," but he figured he'd better not start anything. So he simply said, "Get lost, will you?"

Fortunately, Mr. Rodgers had just entered the cafeteria, and Plug decided it would be smart for him to move on. As he walked away, he mouthed, "I'll get *you* later!"

Before lunch period was over, there was an announcement over the public-address system. Mrs. Goodman, the school secretary, said that school was going to close at one o'clock. The weather bureau was warning people that they should move to higher ground by that night, because they expected the hurricane to hit Black Bayou the next afternoon.

Hurrying home at one o'clock, Bertram found his parents in their office listening to a weather report on the radio. "I suppose they let you out early because of the hurricane," Bertram's mother said. "We've been discussing it, and we've decided to stick it out here."

"Yes," his father agreed. "This building has stood up to a lot of storms over the years. We'll feel safer if we're here to protect our home and our business."

Bertram was surprised by their decision, but he quickly realized there was more to it than just the storm. His parents were afraid of destruction of another kind. They obviously thought that if they left the Fear Factory, Horace Q. Wright would demolish it and they would have nothing to come back to. In fact, the Potters had never left the museum all alone, for just that reason, ever since Horace had become mayor.

When they discussed the decision to remain in the house that evening at dinner, Poppa was

jubilant. It was one of the few times Bertram had ever seen Poppa agree with his parents. But he knew Poppa loved storms, and hurricanes were his favorite.

"Everyone will come up onto the second floor," Bertram's father said calmly. "We'll make up the two beds in the guest room, so that Poppa and Sigmund can sleep there, since there may be a chance of flooding. We can cut the electricity to the first floor if necessary, so we'll be as safe as possible. All the bedrooms are in the back, which is where the storm will be coming from. So, if things get too bad back there, we will camp out on the living room floor."

Bertram was excited. He had never seen a natural disaster before, and he couldn't wait.

The next morning the sky was already scary looking. "My kind of weather!" Poppa said cheerfully, stretching his arms over his head as he walked into the kitchen for breakfast. He had already brought up a supply of clothes and personal articles, books and his magic equipment from his apartment. "Just to make sure," he told Bertram.

But by ten o'clock Poppa was getting restless. He told Bertram not to say anything to his parents, and he headed down to the lab with Sigmund. "I'll be back for lunch," he promised.

Bertram sat and stared out the window of his room, which overlooked the back field. He hadn't closed the shutters yet, but he had put tape on the glass to prevent it from breaking in the wind. He watched the sky get uglier and uglier, and the wind was becoming stronger by the minute.

Even though there was nothing much to watch blowing in the back field — it was almost empty of plants, because his parents considered gardening a frivolous activity — he could tell the wind had picked up a lot of speed. He wondered how much longer it would be until they felt the full effect of the storm. He thought about closing the shutters.

Suddenly he saw a familiar figure out back — and just at that moment, the rain began. The large drops pelted the glass window, and Bertram strained to see through the sheets of water to the field below. He was right — it was The Man Being Boiled Alive out there! Only now he wasn't being boiled, he was being drenched!

Quickly pulling the shutters together and locking them, Bertram went to his closet, pulled on his slicker and hip waders, grabbed a coil of strong rope, and crept downstairs as quietly as he could. Hurrying through the dark corridors of the main floor, he finally came to Poppa's lab.

He quickly rapped out the code, but because of the noise of the wind, he had to repeat it several times before Poppa opened the door.

"He's out there. He's in the back field!" Bertram shouted. Poppa and Siggy looked alarmed.

"I'm going out to get him," Bertram said confidently. "I think he wants to come in from the storm. I know I can get him to come back home!"

"You're as crazy as I am," Poppa said. "I mean, I'm glad, but you can't go out in a hurricane, Bertram! Even I wouldn't do that!"

"*You're* down here in the lab, when you should be upstairs," said Bertram.

"That's different. It's not like being outside. Anyway, we were closing up shop and getting ready to go upstairs."

"I have to get him. You don't understand!" Bertram yelled.

He ran out of the lab and through the corridors that he knew better than anyone else. Racing to a side door, he managed to push it open. Grabbing onto the building for support, he made his way slowly toward the back field. He knew what he was doing was stupid and crazy, but he had to get the creature before it did any more damage.

As Bertram made his way around to the back of the building, he had a hard time standing upright in the swelling wind, and he could hardly see from the pelting rain. But not wanting to be outwitted again by a statue, he steadfastly kept up his pursuit.

When he saw Bertram approaching, The Man Being Boiled Alive backed away, onto a tiny peninsula entirely surrounded by the bayou. Bertram saw him and, crawling now, followed him onto the windswept, wet strip of land.

"Now I've got you!" he shouted at the statue. Bertram tried to make a lasso with the coil of rope he had thrown over his shoulder, but it was too hard to do that and stand up at the same time, because of the wind. Finally, he managed to make a small loop, which he threw at the creature — only to have the wind blow the rope right back in his face.

The statue watched Bertram struggle with the rope, a horrified expression on his tortured face. Before Bertram could check to see whether or not The Man was melting in the torrential rain, he turned around, jumped into the bayou and disappeared from sight.

Bertram groaned. His big chance to catch the statue and bring him back — was *alive* the right word? — and he had blown it! Now he would never find out what had made the statue walk, or why he liked pie so much and if he had used anything like a brain to out-maneuver his pursuers.

Suddenly the realization that he was out in a hurricane hit Bertram hard. Part of him was incredibly excited. There was something bracing about the wind and the rain, and he felt like a hero. He began to understand why Poppa found storms so fascinating.

But the other part of him was scared to death! On the way back to the house the wind was behind him, and Bertram was afraid he would blow away, and land somewhere in Tennessee.

Suddenly Bertram felt a strong arm tug at him. Looking up, he came eye to eye with Poppa, who shook his head sternly. Poppa held onto him and together they struggled back to the building. He and Poppa made their way around to the front entrance, which was sheltered from the wind. Sigmund was waiting there to let them in, and he closed the door quickly after them and bolted it securely.

In the lobby of the Fear Factory, Poppa flung his arms around the sopping-wet Bertram and hugged him for a long time. He didn't have to say anything for his grandson to know how he felt.

"Now, let's take off these wet jackets and get upstairs before your parents notice we're missing!" Poppa said.

"You mean they haven't yet?" Bertram asked, amazed.

"No," Siggy answered. "Zey are very busy vith making some new advertisements for the museum. No vasted moments, yes?"

Bertram giggled as he removed his heavy galoshes. "I'm sorry I didn't catch the creature," he said. "But it was fun, anyway!"

Siggy shook his head. "You are only two people I know who like bad veather."

"Face it, Siggy," Bertram said as he ran upstairs to join his parents. "We're the only two people you know!"

The hurricane blew over without damaging the Fear Factory, and Black Bayou as a whole was saved from the worst of the storm. When school reopened, Bertram told Wesley and Adelaide about how he had chased the statue out in the hurricane. They were both impressed.

But Bertram was still worried about what might happen if The Man Being Boiled Alive ever found his way out of the bayou in back of the Fear Factory. He wondered if he had even survived the huge storm — after all, he was only made of wax.

But Bertram had a feeling the creature was still around — too much so, in fact. Occasionally when he was walking through the hallways of the Factory, he felt as if someone was watching him. Several times he thought he caught a glimpse of The Man Being Boiled Alive staring at him from a dark corner. But when he investigated, the figure was nowhere in sight.

Bertram told his suspicions to Poppa. "It's possible," his grandfather said, "but unlikely."

"It's more than possible," Bertram insisted. "I know the statue is back. Now we may really get a chance to find out what makes him tick. If only he'll let me near him!"

On Friday evening, as Bertram was helping to close up the museum, he came face to face with The Man Being Boiled Alive.

"You think you're so clever!" Bertram yelled at him as he disappeared around a corner and down the hall. "I'll catch you!"

When he went over to Wesley's house that night to watch a movie, Bertram told his friend that he had seen the statue again in the museum.

"I think you're losing your mind," Wesley said. "I read somewhere that being out in a storm can make a person temporarily insane. Or maybe you're just waterlogged."

Bertram rolled his eyes. "I'm telling you, Wes — I've seen him in the Fear Factory. And I'm going to smoke him out."

"How? Are you going to use a stink bomb?" Wesley asked.

"No, no. That was just a figure of speech," Bertram said, exasperated.

"Oh." Wesley shrugged. "Well, if I were you, I'd be worrying more about our next map for social studies. If you recall, we got a C-minus on the last one, that flour and water number."

"That's because you didn't help me and I had to mix up the whole thing by myself — wait! That's it!" Bertram cried excitedly. "Remember how that spoon I was stirring with kept getting stuck in the mixture? That's how I'm going to catch The Man Being Boiled Alive — in plaster of Paris!"

"I'll believe it when I see it," Wesley said dejectedly.

"Good. Come over to my house on Sunday," Bertram told him. "This'll be better than any movie you've ever seen!"

— Twelve —

The next morning, Bertram sold tickets to the Fear Factory until noon. Then, despite his parents' order to stay away, he stole down to Poppa's lab.

"Get out of here!" Poppa said when he answered the door. "This place is off-limits, remember?"

"But Poppa, I had to come. I figured out a way to catch The Man Being Boiled Alive."

"What is this? Did you get brain fever from being out in the storm? You saw the statue jump into the bayou, didn't you?" Poppa asked. "He is gone, finished, kaput."

"I don't know. I thought it would be the end of him that day, too. But I've seen him. He's inside the factory."

Poppa laughed. "Go on!"

"No, I'm serious," Bertram insisted. "And we have to catch him once and for all. I'm surprised nobody else has seen him yet. I wouldn't be surprised if he starts showing up on the tours. And if Mom and Dad find out we had anything to do with this. . . . "

Poppa nodded. "Good point. All right, suppose I do believe you. What is this brilliant plan of yours?"

"Well, first I need you and Sigmund to make a new figure, called the 'Woman Being Boiled Alive.' But please don't add any X-13."

"If you recall, that was never my idea," Poppa reminded Bertram. "Okay, I follow you so far."

"How long will it take to make the statue?" Bertram asked.

"From planning to execution, at least two weeks."

Bertram frowned. "That's way too long. I have to have it by tomorrow."

"Impossible!" Poppa exclaimed. "It cannot be done."

"But Poppa, we're not putting it on display for the general public. It's only for another statue to see. Can't you lower your standards?"

"Well, I suppose so, just this once. You want a statue, the quicker the better and you don't care what it looks like, as long as it's a woman who's in hot water."

"That's right," Bertram said, smiling. "You can leave the rest up to me."

Bertram spent most of Saturday night in the downstairs storeroom preparing a huge vat of plaster of Paris. He calculated how long it would take to get to the right consistency, and then he went to work. By Sunday morning it was perfect.

Poppa and Siggy, meanwhile, were busily at work on the new statue. By using the same mold, with some minor modifications, they were able to pour a woman as grotesque in her own way as The Man. Poppa shuddered when he looked at her crudeness, but Bertram insisted that she would do nicely.

By Sunday morning, she had cooled enough to be moved into the vat of plaster of Paris that was waiting in the storeroom. Bertram's parents went to church at their regular time, and were conveniently out of the way, just as Bertram had planned. Wesley showed up at ten o'clock — he had come over to help so that he could get a good view of the whole thing — and he and Bertram positioned themselves behind a corner in the storeroom where they were hidden from view.

"What if this guy turns on us?" Wesley asked after they had waited in silence for fifteen minutes.

"Just remember, he's only a statue that can move," Bertram reassured him. "He's not a real monster or a killer or anything."

"Yes, but if he eats pie, he could try to eat us."

"Not a chance," Bertram said. "If there was any danger in this plan, do you think I would involve you?"

"Yes," Wesley answered without hesitation.

"I would not," Bertram argued.

"How do you know The Man will come by?"

"He will. Don't worry."

The boys didn't have to wait more than a half hour. "Shhh," Bertram whispered, interrupting a story Wesley was telling about his trip to Baton Rouge during the hurricane. "I hear something coming," he warned Wesley.

"I don't," Wesley whispered back.

"Remember, I have the hearing of a bat," Bertram responded.

Sure enough, The Man Being Boiled Alive came into view a few moments later. Bertram couldn't help feeling almost sad that the statue's days were about to end.

The Man stopped before the woman standing in the vat of plaster of Paris as if he had come upon a great discovery. For a few moments he just stood in front of her, as if he was fascinated by her beauty — or lack thereof, Bertram thought. It seemed that even statues had feelings of some sort.

Then The Man stepped forward. When he got just in front of the vat he hesitated, then stepped right into the gooey mess with his female friend. As he did so, he triggered an electric eye that Bertram had set up, and a huge piece of muslin came down from the ceiling and landed on The Man's head. The creature was so surprised that he didn't realize that the harder he struggled with the cloth, the deeper he was setting himself in the cement.

Bertram and Wesley ran up with a huge coil of rope, which they tightened around the struggling statue. Wesley looked as if he was about to be sick, but he gallantly helped Bertram secure the rope around the oozing figure.

Bertram took another length of rope out of his pocket and tied it to the rope around The Man Being Boiled Alive. Then he tied the other end to a strong pillar in the middle of the room. When he was sure it was fastened securely, he told Wesley to stand guard while he ran to get Poppa.

"Well?" Poppa asked expectantly when Bertram ran in the door, panting.

"Success!" Bertram cried. "We've got him in the plaster, just like I'd hoped," he gasped. "But I've been thinking about it, and I think the best thing to do is to melt down the statue."

Poppa looked into Bertram's eyes. "Do you really think we have to?" he asked. "I worked so hard on him, and he turned out to be such a nice man, after all."

"I know, Poppa. But as much as I'd like to find out how the X-13 worked, if we take him out of that plaster of Paris, who knows what will happen? We can't take that risk again."

Poppa let out a loud sigh. "As usual, you are right. But I've never had to destroy one of my creations before — it hurts."

"Don't worry. We'll make lots more," Bertram promised.

A short while later, Poppa and Sigmund arrived at the storeroom pushing a huge cart with an extra-large pot full of boiling water on it. With mitts on their hands, the four of them carefully hoisted the pot into the air and tossed it at The Man Being Boiled Alive.

The first layer of his wax skin started to slide off, and he was instantly turned into a shorter version of himself. "Poppa," Siggy said, "do you think it is hurting?"

"I give you my word — he isn't feeling a thing," Poppa answered in a solemn voice.

Siggy returned to the lab for another pot of boiling water, and after they had doused The Man again, he collapsed into a liquid that was half wax and half plaster. Poppa and Siggy wheeled the whole exhibit into the lab to finish the job of melting both statues down to nothing.

"This is such a shame," Poppa said with a huge sigh. "The discovery of the century, and I can't even share it with the rest of the world."

Bertram was sad, too. Taking the life of the statue made him feel a little like a murderer, even though he knew he had done the right thing. "It was only half a discovery, though," he reminded Poppa, hoping it would ease some of his guilt, too. "We didn't know how to control him. I think we were pretty lucky he only had food and women on his mind. He could have gotten us closed down for good, if he had known how to talk!"

"That's for sure," Poppa said with a smile. "I'll get rid of the rest of the X-13 so that there's no chance of another piece of wax walking around Black Bayou telling everyone what we're up to."

"Are you sure you have to do that?" Wesley asked. "Couldn't we try it just once more — on a less tortured figure, maybe?"

Poppa shook his head. "No more. Not now. But maybe one day, when I figure out how to control the stuff, we'll see what we can cook up for our friend Mr. Horace Q. Wright. If we play our cards right, we might be able to send him packing forever. After all, who would believe him if he came up with another story about a walking statue?"

Bertram chuckled. "Sometimes the truth is the hardest thing to believe."

"Especially when it comes from a family of crackpots," Poppa said with a wink as he gave

Bertram an affectionate squeeze on the shoulder.

"You can say that again!" Wesley agreed. "I just hope my mother doesn't ask what I did over here today."

"I know — let's drink a toast in memory of The Man Being Boiled Alive," Bertram said.

"I have some grape juice in my ice box," Siggy said. "Oh, this is a vonderful idea!" He returned a few minutes later carrying four small plastic cups and a quart jar of juice. He poured the juice quickly and handed it around.

"To The Man Being Boiled Alive — we're sorry it had to come to this!" Wesley said, striking a dramatic pose.

"No, no — to The Man Being Boiled Alive, may you never fall into a bowl of soup!" Siggy cried. He burst out laughing, which was something he almost never did.

But Wesley shook his head. "To Poppa," he said, "for creating the X-13 and making it all happen."

"And to Bertram," Poppa replied, raising his glass, "for getting us all into this mess!"

They all took a swig of juice and Bertram tossed his cup over his shoulder into the vat that had once contained The Man Being Boiled Alive. What he didn't see was the hand that caught it . . .

Don't miss the next thrilling, chilling book in the FEAR FACTORY series, when Bertram and Poppa bring Bertram's great-great-grandfather BACK FROM THE GRAVE!

When Poppa Potter decides to conjure up the ghost of his grandfather, Pygmalion Potter, Bertram thinks it's a terrific idea. He loves to hear Poppa's stories of Pygmalion's pranks, and now he'll actually be able to meet the old man — if Poppa's plans work out, that is.

But at the Fear Factory, anything can happen and usually does. Sure enough, when Pygmalion's spirit does show up, Poppa, Bertram, Wesley, and Adelaide get more than they had bargained for.

Pygmalion is a lot of fun at first, and Bertram and Poppa are enjoying every minute of his visit — until Pygmalion starts meddling with the waxworks and playing practical jokes on Horace Q. Wright, Black Bayou's stuffy mayor. Suddenly the whole Potter family is in big trouble, and Poppa decides it's time for Pygmalion to go back where he came from.

But Pygmalion has other ideas. He's having such a good time that he doesn't want to return to "the other side" ever! Poppa and Bertram have to figure out a way to get rid of him before the gleeful ghost finishes the Fear Factory once and for all!